PRAISE FOR THE *DRAMA HIGH* SERIES

"The teen drama is center-court Compton, with enough plots and sub-plots to fill a few episodes of any reality show."
—*Ebony* magazine on *Drama High: Courtin' Jayd*

"Abundant, juicy drama."
—*Kirkus Reviews* on *Drama High: Holidaze*

"You'll definitely feel for Jayd Jackson, the bold sixteen-year-old Compton, California, junior at the center of the keep-it-real *Drama High* stories."
—*Essence* magazine on *Drama High: Jayd's Legacy*

"Edged with comedy and a provoking street-savvy plot line, Compton native and *Drama High* author L. Divine writes a fascinating story capturing the voice of young black America."
—*The Cincinnati Herald* on the *Drama High* series

"Filled with all the elements that make for a good book—young love, non-stop drama and a taste of the supernatural, it is sure to please."
—THE RAWSISTAZ REVIEWERS on *Drama High: The Fight*

"If you grew up on a steady diet of saccharine–*Sweet Valley* novels and think there aren't enough books specifically for African-American teens, you're in luck."
—*The Prince George's Sentinel* on *Drama High: The Fight*

"Through a healthy mix of book smarts, life experiences ~ ~ down-to-earth flavor, L. Divine h~ coming-of-age tale for African-Am∈
—*The Atlanta Voice* on *Dra*

Also by L. Divine

THE FIGHT

SECOND CHANCE

JAYD'S LEGACY

FRENEMIES

LADY J

COURTIN' JAYD

HUSTLIN'

KEEP IT MOVIN'

HOLIDAZE

CULTURE CLASH

COLD AS ICE

PUSHIN'

THE MELTDOWN

Published by Kensington Publishing Corporation

Drama High, Vol. 14

SO, SO HOOD

L. DIVINE

Dafina KTeen Books
KENSINGTON PUBLISHING CORP.
www.kensingtonbooks.com/KTeen

DAFINA KTEEN BOOKS are published by

Kensington Publishing Corp.
119 West 40th Street
New York, NY 10018

All Kensington titles, imprints and distributed lines are available at special quantity discounts for bulk purchases for sales promotion, premiums, fund-raising, educational or institutional use.

Special book excerpts or customized printings can also be created to fit specific needs. For details, write or phone the office of the Kensington Special Sales Manager: Attn. Special Sales Department. Kensington Publishing Corp., 119 West 40th Street, New York, NY 10018. Phone: 1-800-221-2647.

K logo Reg. US Pat. & TM Off.
Sunburst logo Reg. US Pat. & TM Off.

ISBN-13: 978-0-7582-3119-2
ISBN-10: 0-7582-3119-9

First Printing: June 2011

10 9 8 7 6 5 4 3 2 1

Printed in the United States of America

ACKNOWLEDGMENTS

Thank you to my mom, Dorothy Lynette, for my flyy, nearly illegible handwriting, which has become a large part of my brand.

To my favorite AME church folks: Pastor Jewell Holloway, Pastor Benjamin Thomas, Pastor Clyde Odem, my grandmother, Dorothy Jean Harvey, and to the black church in general. I feel blessed to have come through such a revolutionary spiritual organization that has paved the road for the woman I am today. Thank you very much for providing a forum for me and my predecessors to thrive.

To everyone at Dafina/Kensington books for publishing my series. To Liz Jote for your consistent support.

To the Dojang for positively changing me and my children's lives forever. And to Kamay Franklin for always.

And to everyone who believed in both L. Divine and *Drama High* from its inception: It's been a long, challenging road and we've only just begun. Thank you for sharing in this faithful journey.

THE CREW

Jayd

A sassy seventeen-year-old from Compton, California, who comes from a long line of Louisiana conjure women. She is the only one in her lineage born with brown eyes and a caul. Her grandmother appropriately named her "Jayd," which is also the name her grandmother took on in her days as a voodoo queen in New Orleans. Jayd now lives in her mother's apartment in Inglewood. She visits her grandmother on the weekends in Compton, her former home. Jayd is in all AP classes. She has a tense relationship with her father, whom she sees occasionally, and has never-ending drama in her life, whether at school or home.

Mama/Lynn Mae

When Jayd gets in over her head, her grandmother, Mama, is always there to help her. A full-time conjure woman with magical green eyes and a long list of both clients and haters, Mama also serves as Jayd's teacher, confidante, and protector.

Mom/Lynn Marie

At thirtysomething years old, Lynn Marie would never be mistaken for a mother of a teenager. Jayd's mom is definitely all that and with her green eyes, she keeps the men guessing. Able to talk to Jayd telepathically, Lynn Marie is always there when Jayd needs her.

Netta

The owner of Netta's Never Nappy Beauty Shop, Netta is Mama's best friend, business partner, and godsister in their religion. She also serves as a godmother to Jayd, who works part-time at Netta's Shop.

Esmeralda

Mama's nemesis and Jayd's nightmare, this next-door neighbor is anything but friendly. She relocated to Compton from Louisiana around the same time Mama did and has been a thorn in Mama's side ever since. She continuously causes trouble for Mama and Jayd. Esmeralda's cold blue eyes have powers of their own, although not nearly as powerful as Mama's.

Rah

Rah is Jayd's first love from junior high school, who has come back into her life when a mutual friend, Nigel, transfers from Rah's high school (Westingle) to South Bay. He knows everything about her and is her spiritual confidant. Rah lives in Los Angeles but grew up with his grandparents in Compton like Jayd. He loves Jayd fiercely but has a baby mama who refuses to go away. Rah is a hustler by necessity and a music producer by talent. He takes care of his younger brother, Kamal, and holds the house down while his dad is locked up and his mother strips at a local club.

Misty

The word "frenemies" was coined for this former best friend of Jayd's. Misty has made it her mission to sabotage Jayd any way she can. Living around the corner from Jayd, she has the unique advantage of being an original hater from the neighborhood and at school.

KJ

He's the most popular basketball player on campus, Jayd's ex-boyfriend, and Misty's current boyfriend. Ever since he and Jayd broke up, he's made it his personal mission to per-secute her.

Nellie
One of Jayd's best friends, Nellie is the prissy princess of the crew. She is also dating Chance, even though it's Nigel she's really feeling. Nellie made history at South Bay by becoming the first black Homecoming princess and has let the crown go to her head.

Mickey
The gangster girl of Jayd's small crew, she and Nellie are best friends but often at odds with each other, mostly because Nellie secretly wishes she could be more like Mickey. A true hood girl, she loves being from Compton, and her ex-man with no name is a true gangster. Mickey and Nigel have quickly become South Bay High's newest couple.

Jeremy
A first for Jayd, Jeremy is her white on again/off again boyfriend who also happens to be the most popular cat at South Bay. Rich, tall, and extremely handsome, Jeremy's witty personality and good conversation keep Jayd on her toes and give Rah a run for his money—literally.

Mickey's Man
Never using his name, Mickey's original boyfriend is a trouble-maker and always hot on Mickey's trail. Always in and out of jail, Mickey's man is notorious in her hood for being a coldhearted gangster, and loves to be in control. He also has a thing for Jayd, but Jayd can't stand to be anywhere near him.

Nigel

The new quarterback on the block, Nigel is a friend of Jayd's from junior high and also Rah's best friend, making Jayd's world even smaller at South Bay High. Nigel is the star football player and dumped his ex-girlfriend at Westingle (Tasha) to be with his new baby-mama-to-be, Mickey. Jayd is caught up in the mix as a friend to them both, but her loyalty lies with Nigel because she's known him longer and he's always had her back.

Chance

The rich, white hip-hop kid of the crew, Chance is Jayd's drama homie and Nellie's boyfriend, if you let him tell it. He used to have a crush on Jayd and now has turned his attention to Nellie for the time being. Chance's dreams of being black come true when he discovers he was adopted. His biological mother is half black, and his birth name is Chase.

Bryan

The youngest of Mama's children and Jayd's favorite uncle, Bryan is a dj by night and works at the local grocery store during the day. He's also an acquaintance of both Rah and KJ from playing ball around the hood. Bryan often gives Jayd helpful advice about her problems with boys and hating girls alike. Out of all of Jayd's uncles, Bryan gives her grandparents the least amount of trouble.

Jay

Jay is more like an older brother to Jayd than her cousin. He lives with Mama, but his mother (Mama's youngest daughter, Anne) left him when he was a baby and never returned. He doesn't know his father and attends Compton High. He and Jayd often cook together and help Mama around the house.

Jayd's Journal

As strange as it may sound, my initiation two weeks ago was my marriage to my spiritual mother, Oshune. Mama says there's nothing like being an iyawo—a wife to my head orisha. Mama explains it as the most important relationship I'll ever have. Now, my head as well as my heart belongs to Oshune, and because her love and devotion knows no boundaries she also belongs to me. According to Mama, as my days as a newborn were short and sweet so is my time as iyawo—not only because everyone dotes on me, but also because it's the most sensitive I'll ever be—spiritually, mentally, and physically. Maybe that's why my emotions are running wild over seeing a picture of Jeremy kissing Cameron. I can't think or dream about anything else since seeing the texted photo yesterday.

The beautiful, handmade journal Mama and Netta presented me with to keep a record of my first year as a priestess is supposed to be filled with my spiritual transformation, not the same old shit regarding trifling dudes and the females they roll with. Instead of writing about my latest dream or other surreal experience while dressed in white from head to toe, I'm writing about my man's indiscretions. I wonder if all newlyweds worry about their cheating boyfriends during the honeymoon phase of their blossoming love?

Jeremy's already left several messages to let me know he's on his way home and wants to visit as soon as possible, but I'm not sure if he wants to see me like this. So much has changed this summer and it's more than my attire. I don't know if anything will ever go back to the way it was before, but what I do know is that the truth is coming out sooner than later—the good, the bad, and the hood.

Prologue

After my shopping excursion with my crew abruptly ended yesterday afternoon with me plotting ways to kill Jeremy and Cameron once their plane lands on American soil, I went back to Mama's house and took a long, cool bath. It's more dangerous now than ever for my head to get too hot. If I have a dream about Queen Califia, Maman or another one of my powerful ancestors breaking someone down with their gift of sight, I'm liable to bring it back with me when I wake up. I might not be able to control myself when I look into Jeremy's eyes and he denies anything's going on with his side trick when I have the physical evidence to prove otherwise. Jeremy's crippled mind is the last thing I need on my conscience right now.

My initiation has made my dreams more intense and my sight off the chain, but it's still in the beginning stages. But so far seeing my dreams come to fruition is the most natural feeling ever—just like breathing. I've decided to tell Rah about my dream of his baby mama Sandy's untimely insemination by another dude and not him. She can try and lie if she wants to, but I know the real story and she needs to come correct here and now. Rah couldn't join us at the mall yesterday so we all decided to meet up at his place since his crazy baby mama Sandy is MIA for the afternoon. Knowing Sandy, she won't be missing for long, so we'd better enjoy the peace while it lasts because when she gets back I'm going straight for the jugular.

"Your mama's a total bitch," Mickey says, throwing the cloth diaper with remnants of baby formula down on the table in front of the futon. So much for a chill session vibing to Rah and Nigel's latest beats. I remember when the garage-turned-studio was the most serene place we could all hang together. Now it's yet another firing post for our collective drama.

"Mickey, the baby," Nigel says, caressing Nickey's soft hair. She's the only one who can get any rest in here. That girl can fall asleep anywhere. Staying asleep seems to be her main problem.

"Nickey knows her mama's telling the truth about that evil woman," Mickey says, sitting in the chair next to the table. She looks better and she's back to her old self. As soon as I put some color on I'm checking Misty's ass for giving Mickey the unhealthy vitamins Mama's nemesis, Esmeralda, prescribed to make Mickey lose weight and her mind. For now I'll have to settle for Dr. Whitmore expertly switching the tainted pills with his healing combination in time enough to save my vain friend. The last thing our crew needs is Mickey wigging out under Esmeralda's influence. The girl's already a handful and then some.

"She's still my mom," Nigel says, reading the sports section of the newspaper at the work desk he and Rah share. Rah's busy counting his cash. He's been hustling harder than ever since his mom stopped chipping in for the rent and bills. But from the frustrated look across Rah's brow, I'd say he's still coming up short.

"She ain't right, Nigel," Mickey sourly reiterates.

I wouldn't call Mrs. Esop a bitch, but she's not the nicest

woman in the world. I've yet to face her after ducking out early from the debutante ball and I know she's waiting patiently for an explanation. But what can I say? I never wanted to do it anyway. It's ironic how the universe has a way of working out no matter how much we try and plan otherwise.

"What happened now?" I ask, leaning across the futon and touching my goddaughter's toes. If she's dreaming I want her to feel my presence and know that I've got her back, consciously and subconsciously. Rah's daughter, Rahima, looks up at me from her spot on the carpet where she's surrounded by toys and smiles knowing I've got her, too.

"Since I've been staying at Rah's house for the past couple of weeks she's convinced my dad to cut off my allowance, saying I'm not earning it because I'm not home to do my chores."

"That's a cold move right there," I say, ever surprised at the depth of Mrs. Esop's swag. She knows she's a lot of woman to deal with and uses it to her advantage all day long.

"A bitch, Jayd. There's no other way around that shit." Mickey keeps it real all the time, damn the audience. "We're supposed to be saving up for our own place, but now we ain't got a damned thing to save." Nigel and Mickey aren't even married yet and Mickey's already claiming his money. We all know Mickey's not making any cheddar of her own.

"For real, Mickey—in front of my daughter, too?" Rah asks, looking up from his stacks of tens and twenties at Rahima stacking her blocks like they're money. He'd better be careful of the example he sets for baby girl, too. "Unlike your newborn, Rahima's talking and can repeat what she hears."

Like her mama's any better. If Rahima wanted to curse by now she'd be a professional with the example she's got in Sandy. But I'm with Rah—not swearing around the little ones is best.

"I don't want to have to up my game, but our hustle's all

I've got now." Nigel looks at his boy and Rah recognizes the hunger in his eyes. They go way back to elementary school before Rah's dad went to prison. Nigel and his family were there for Rah when he had no parents at home or food in the fridge and now it's Rah's turn to return the love.

"Y'all can move in with me," Rah says, throwing the last bill on the pile and leaning back in his seat. "Kamal's spending more time at my grandparents' house and me and Rahima can chill in the den while you, Mickey, and the baby take my room."

"For real, Rah?" Mickey asks in disbelief.

It's not exactly what they had in mind, but it'll have to do. Living with Rah is much better than sharing a room with her little sister and a bathroom with everyone else in her crowded household. There are two and a half bathrooms in this house—a good ratio for six people. That's the thing I miss most about being at my mom's apartment, but I can't go back there until my time in whites is over. Luckily it ends right before school starts, allowing me privacy to create my first day back look. I want to start my senior year off as flyy as possible.

"Man, I don't know," Nigel says, shaking his head. "If Sandy's living here, it's going to be tough."

"That won't be a problem much longer, I'm sure," I say.

My friends look at me wondering what I know, but I'm not giving up anything until Sandy gets here. I want to see Sandy's face when I confront her with the truth about her insane ways.

"Man, we'll work it out," Rah says. "Besides, I could use some help. My mom's been slipping on the rent lately. I should change the locks, but I can't since it's her house and all."

Rah's mom is hardly ever here and only shows up to borrow money and weed from Rah. Sandy's just like her, explaining Rah's save-a-ho attitude, but I firmly believe that some broads should be left out in the cold.

"All right then, man," Nigel says, putting his hand out for his boy who returns the gesture. "I'll get our stuff tomorrow. And here's something to make it official." Nigel pulls out five one-hundred-dollar bills from his pocket and hands them to Rah. Houses in this neighborhood cost way more than that, but I know Rah's grandparents actually own the house and only charge his mom about half of what it would normally cost to live here.

"Bet," Rah says, making Mickey's day. "Now can we get this Saturday session officially started? We can leave the girls in here and move to the living room. I don't know about y'all, but I could go for a pizza or three."

Sounds like a good plan to me. I'm glad our crew is somewhat back to normal even if Nellie's presence is missed. She's too busy hanging with her new friend from church, David, who I'm convinced just wants to get in her panties, but I have to handle one broad at a time. Sandy's first on the list, and then Cameron. The poor white girl won't know what hit her by the time I'm through. If she thinks I'm giving up my man without a fight she's got another think coming. Unfortunately for Cameron, she picked the wrong boyfriend to jock. No matter where she and Jeremy are from, in my hood if you want a man who's already spoken for, you have to be willing to deal with the consequences. And I'm just the one to teach the trick how we do things in Compton.

~ 1 ~
Come Again?

I don't care if you don't want me/
'Cause I'm yours, yours, yours anyhow.

—JAY HAWKINS

Not wasting any time, Mickey has taken all of Sandy's things out of the room formerly known as Rah's and put them in the hallway. Rah advised against it, but once Mickey gets started there's no stopping her. I feel sorry for Rahima and Nickey. Both of their mothers are forces to be reckoned with and with them living under the same roof it's going to be a new storm every day. That's why as their godmother I owe it to them to check the hussy once and for all. I just hope Rah sides with me instead of with his sympathetic heart for Sandy's bull.

"What's up with y'all?" Sandy asks, stepping into the foyer and interrupting Mickey's moving session. She couldn't have timed her return any better. It's time to shut Sandy down and Mickey's already started the process for me.

"Rah, what's this heffa doing with my shit?" she asks, stepping over her clothes strewn all over the floor and eyeing Mickey hard. After all the trouble I went through to get rid of the broad for Rah and his daughter's sake, I still can't believe he let Sandy stay here again in the first place. I don't know what kind of spell she's got my boy under, but I'm just the sistah to break it.

"She and Nigel are living here now, Sandy. You have to take the couch until you can find somewhere else to stay," Rah says, almost sounding sad about his decision to put her ass in the living room. What the hell?

Mickey walks back into the bedroom to get more stuff and Sandy looks on in amazement. I bet she never thought this day would come, but it's here and she'd better recognize there's a new queen of this castle.

"Rah, are you shitting me?" Sandy asks, collecting her lingerie, boots, and other work clothes from the floor. "I'm pregnant with your baby, fool, and this is how you treat me?"

Rah's silence speaks volumes, and I don't have time to let her manipulate the situation any further. Thank God I'm not Rah's girlfriend anymore because I'd have to fight for him every day. Who, other than Sandy's Amazonian ass, has that kind of energy?

"Sandy, it's over," I say, moving from the couch to the foyer and letting it all hang out. I turn around to face an exhausted Rah standing by the front door. I don't need my mother's powers to cool his mind. What I'm about to reveal from one of my recent dreams is enough to freeze everyone in the room. "Sandy slept with Trish's brother, your supplier, Rah. And this is his baby, not yours."

The truth settles in the still air like a quiet fart; no one saw it coming, but everyone's painfully aware of its presence.

"She's a liar," Sandy says, completely busted.

Nigel and Rah look at each other knowing this shit ain't good. Trish's brother supplies them both with the only steady income either of them have and they can't afford to have any beef with that dude, especially not over Sandy's trifling ass.

"Get to stepping, trick," Mickey says, throwing more of Sandy's things on the floor, which pisses Sandy off even more. Sandy charges for Mickey, who doesn't back down for a minute.

"Stop it, now!" Rah yells, holding Sandy back while Nigel gets his girl. What a mess. But as Mama says, real change rarely comes easy.

"Get your stuff and bounce, Sandy," I say, glad she has no more power over Rah, or so I think.

"Not so fast," Rah says, looking from me to Mickey and Nigel. "Like I said, Sandy, you can stay here until you work something else out. But don't get too comfortable. And I'll check with Trish to see if that nigga knows about you carrying his seed." Rah lets Sandy go and she heads toward the bedroom with some of her belongings in tow. Luckily the babies are sleeping peacefully in the den, but not for long if we keep this up all night.

"Come again?" I ask as my neck snaps to the right on its own accord. Even my body can't believe what I just heard. "Why do you need to call your ex-girlfriend to verify the story when I just told you the truth, so help me Oshune?" I ask, fully offended. Rah and the rest of our crew should know that my confessions come from a much higher source.

I follow Rah into the kitchen as Nigel and Mickey continue to calm down in the foyer. This new living situation is too hood, even for me, and I've been subjected to bull all my life.

"Jayd, Sandy's got a drug problem. I can't just let her back out on the streets," Rah says, pounding his fist on the kitchen counter. "What am I supposed to tell Rahima when she grows up and finds out I let her mother get strung out?" Rah takes out a cup and fills it with bottled water before drinking it down in one gulp.

"You didn't let Sandy's grown ass do anything but take advantage of your kindness, Rah. Now it's time to let her deal with her own madness."

"I'm not a punk, Jayd. I'm just trying to do the right thing." I look at Rah and attempt to navigate around his fragile ego, but there's no getting around it. He has a weak spot for Sandy because he thinks he can save her from her demons unlike his mother, Carla, who's too far gone to help.

"The right thing for who, because this is certainly the wrong thing for your daughter," I say. "Sandy's no longer your responsibility. Rah, you have to let her go."

Seeing my vehemence for the situation, Rah finally comes to his senses and recognizes that I'm right. Even if his ego is suffering, he has to know Sandy took advantage of him in the worst possible way and that shit can't be tolerated any longer.

When Sandy comes back into the foyer to collect more of her things Rah heads her way and I'm right behind him.

"Sandy, you have to get out. Tonight," Rah says, pointing to her stuff. "And Rahima's staying with me so don't even think about trying to take her out of this house." Finally, Rah mans up and it's about time.

"But Rah, we haven't had a DNA test yet," Sandy says, defeated. "I know you're not kicking me out like this. Where are we supposed to go?" Sandy asks, rubbing on her stomach for dramatic effect.

"What you and your new baby daddy do with that baby is none of my business," Rah says, pointing at Sandy's flabby belly. I know he feels for her, but he feels for Rahima more now that he knows the new baby isn't his.

"But I told you, this is your baby no matter what that witch says," Sandy says, pointing at me.

The heat in my head flusters my cheeks; now the shit's personal.

"I told you about calling me that word, Sandy," I say, tightening the white wrap covering my head, ready to defend my lineage as always. I'm forbidden from any type of altercation, but it's impossible to avoid in my life, especially when heffas like Sandy go too far.

"Oh, my bad. I meant bitch." Sandy's crossed the line yet again and we all know it's her way of trying to hold on to what she's lost, but it's over for her.

"Get out, now," Rah says, opening the front door.

Sandy had better hurry and collect her shit or it's going to be on the front porch from the way Mickey's eyeing the remaining piles.

"But Rah," Sandy pleads. I think she'd better call Trish's brother and see if she can stay with them because this house is closed to her.

"Bitch, he said leave. That's our room now," Mickey says, pointing toward the bedrooms.

"This ain't got shit to do with you, Mickey, so sit down and shut up before I shut you up," Sandy says. Little does she know Mickey's been holding herself back from fighting for almost a year while she was pregnant and is ready to get live with the best of them.

"Look here," Mickey says, removing one oversized, gold hoop from her earlobe and then the other. "I don't know who the hell you think you're dealing with, but I don't give a damn about you or your little baby, if you're really pregnant."

Sandy looks shocked as Mickey continues to remove her jewelry, obviously ready to throw the first blow if need be. If Nellie were here, she'd tell Sandy all about Mickey's love of fighting. That's how they became best friends in the first place. Nellie's too cute to get dirty and Mickey loves a good brawl, making them the perfect cute crew of two before they met me.

"Nigel, check your trick before she gets her ass beat down, for real." Sandy looks on as neither of our boys move an inch. Mickey's got this and we all know it.

"The only trick getting a beat down tonight is you."

Mickey approaches Sandy who steps back at my girl's advance. I guess Sandy does have some good sense left after all.

"Whatever," Sandy says, nervously gathering her things from the floor. "I'm tired of this whack-ass scene anyway." Sandy rolls her eyes at Mickey, who smiles victoriously knowing she can still put fear in a female. Sandy then takes out her cell and dials a number—hopefully to call a taxi. The quicker she's out of here the better for us all.

"You've got ten minutes," Rah says, leading the procession to the den where everyone but Sandy follows. I wave bye to Sandy for what I hope will be the last time before heading to the den with my crew.

"There goes my baby," Usher sings from my cell. I answer Jeremy's call without thinking. I need to change his ringtone because that song's out of date for our relationship.

"Baby, I'm back," Jeremy says like he's all innocent and shit. I've been waiting for this moment for weeks and now that it's here I don't know which emotion to honor first, but it seems like my anger knows exactly what to do.

"I can't talk to you right now, Jeremy. I'm in the middle of something," I say without so much as a hello or good-bye. I can hear Jeremy's shock through the phone, but I don't care how rude I'm being. If I had the time, I'd be much more offensive, so he should consider himself lucky.

"Jayd, Jayd," Jeremy yells through the phone as I close the pink lid. I erase Jeremy's name in my contact list and replace it with the words "Do not answer" to remind me I'm not speaking to him, just in case I should forget. If Jeremy thinks I'm going to be a fool for him, he'd better think again. Like Rah, the new and improved Jayd Jackson is no one's punk. Maybe my previous story line was different, but this is an entirely new and stronger me—damn the bull. Just like Sandy, Mickey, and Nigel, it's time to move on and try something dif-

ferent and that's exactly what I'm going to do with my relationship, too.

Today's officially moving day for Nigel and Mickey and
we're all pitching in to help our friends get settled, even if it
is the last Monday afternoon we'll have to ourselves this summer. My job is to keep an eye on the babies who are inside
sleeping the afternoon away and I'm loving every minute of
it. I know it's strange for some of my friends to be parents
going into our senior year of high school, but that's how it is
sometimes. We've got one more week before school starts
and we intend on enjoying it as much as possible. This summer has flown by, but it's been a good one—minus all the
drama, not to mention my so-called boyfriend's unfaithful
ways.

My phone's been ringing all day and I'm tired of recharg-
ing it, like I'm doing now while sitting on the porch watching
the dudes carry stuff in. Jeremy's been back for a week and
I'm still not talking to him. Other than "go to hell and take
your new chick with you," I don't have too much else to say.
I know I should answer one of his hundreds of messages, but
until I have all my facts straight I don't want to say too much.

"I think that's the end of this load," Nigel says, wiping the
sweat from his brow as he heads inside to take a smoke break
with Rah while they wait for Mickey to return. He looks at
Rah in the living room behind me who shakes his head at the
amount of shit Nigel and Mickey have, and they still have one
more load from Mickey's house they're waiting on. I wonder
where they're going to put the baby's stuff?

"You think?" Rah says, half laughing at our boy. We know
Nigel's been spoiled all his life, but damn.

Nigel's bedroom at his parents' house is easily double the
size of Rah's living room. Nigel didn't even move half of his

belongings, but between he and Mickey they have enough clothes, shoes, and other accessories to fill a boutique.

"Just in time," Nigel says as Chance's car rounds the corner, which we can hear before we see. His sound system is tight—no doubt—but needs to be lowered in Rah's quiet, Windsor Hills neighborhood. The elders around here will call the police on us in a minute for being in violation of their community ordinance, even if we are a stone's throw away from South Central L.A.

Chance pulls up to the curb in front of Rah's house with a passenger, but it's not Nellie. What the hell?

"What up, my peeps?" Chance asks, exiting his Chevy Nova in a pair of gray Abercrombie and Fitch sweats with a white T, and a matching gray and white golf cap. He's looking good and as low-key as a rich boy from Palos Verdes can get to help his homeboy move.

"Jeremy, what are you doing here?" I ask, not sure how to react. I miss my man and am flattered by his persistence, but I'm still fuming about the Cameron situation. I knew the broad was sneaking on the low to get at my boyfriend. Had I been in my right mind, I could've prevented the shit. But unfortunately, the thought of Jeremy touching that broad is etched into my permanent memory and no matter how fine he is, that's all I can see.

"I'm here to see my girlfriend since—for some reason— she won't answer any of my calls," Jeremy says, exiting Chance's car looking as delicious as I remember in his black Adidas shorts and navy tank top. I look down at my white-on-white attire and back up at Jeremy as he and Chance both approach the driveway. They look equally interested in my outfit, but it's Jeremy who asks the question. "Why are you dressed like a nun?"

"It's a spiritual thing," I say, answering in my usual tone

when people ask about my new look as they often do. I couldn't imagine going through a year of this like most iya-wos do. Thank God, Mama has mercy on me.

Chance walks up to Nigel's car parked in the driveway and smiles at our reunion, but it's not all sweet. I stand up and eye Jeremy from the top of the three steps, folding my arms across my chest so he knows I'm not waiting on him with open arms.

Jeremy walks over to me and I brace myself for the impact of his strong arms and clean, seawater scent. "I've missed you, baby," Jeremy says, embracing me tightly, but I refuse to get caught up in the rapture no matter how tempted I may be. Noticing my distance, Jeremy pulls back without letting go of me completely and looks down at my scowl. "What's up with you?"

"I don't know," I say, pushing Jeremy away after allowing him to hold me one second too long. I have to stay strong and I have just the thing to help. I reach over to the banister where my phone is charging and retrieve it for the incriminating evidence. "Just wondering why my boyfriend had to go to another country to cheat on me. There are plenty of willing tricks right here in Southern California to choose from. Oh, but wait, you did choose one from around the way."

I flip the phone open and scroll through the few pictures I have on this thing, mostly of my godbabies and Jeremy and I during happier times.

"Jayd, I don't know what you're talking about," Jeremy says, feigning innocence as I search through my cell for the picture of him and Cameron locking lips in London. As many times as I've viewed the image, I should've made it my screen saver by now. I stop at the photo as Jeremy tries to hug me again.

"Exhibit A, your dishonor," I say, blocking his next advance with the evidence.

Jeremy takes the cell phone from my hand and stares at the photo as if it's new to him. How can it be when it's obviously him and his traveling companion as intimate as legally allowed in public?

"Jayd, I don't know what you think this is, but it's not what it looks like," Jeremy says, turning two shades whiter than he already is. Jeremy's been away so long he's lost his natural beach glow.

Chance looks over his boy's shoulder and then snatches up the phone, staring hard at the picture just like I did when it first came through. I still can't believe my eyes, but truth is truth and pictures don't lie.

"Girl, where'd you get this?" Chance asks, looking for the sender but like me, he has no luck retrieving the information.

"What difference does it make?" I ask, reclaiming the phone from my friend and closing it. "How can you deny kissing Cameron when the proof is right in front of you?"

Jeremy looks at me, unsure of what to say. He's probably trying to think of a good lie to get him out of this shit, but no such luck.

"Jayd, I don't care what that picture looks like, I'm telling you it's not real," Jeremy says, touching my shoulder. Luckily I'm covered from head to toe and can't feel his soft, freshly scented skin against mine. If I could, my defenses would probably drop like they usually do for the men I love.

"What kind of fool do you take me for, Jeremy?" I ask, removing his hand, fully pissed. "It's one thing to deny your wrongdoing, but to tell me that my eyes are lying is a whole other thing."

I look at Chance who doesn't know what to say. What he assumes to be Nellie's infidelity is still fresh on his mind. Otherwise, I'm sure he'd chime in on Jeremy's behalf.

"Hey, what's going on out here?" Nigel asks, smelling like an ashtray and sweating like a pig.

"Jeremy thinking I'm a damned fool, that's what." I stare down at my man who still looks shell-shocked by my attitude. If I didn't know better I'd say he's telling the truth, but unfortunately I've been around too many good liars in my short seventeen years.

Nigel looks at the three of us in amazement. I bet he didn't expect that answer, but that's exactly how I feel.

Jeremy reaches for my right cheek with the tip of his left index finger and I pull back, refusing to let him touch me again.

"Jayd, how long are you going to be mad at me for something I didn't do?"

"How can you deny kissing Cameron when you just saw what we all saw?" I ask, now screaming at Jeremy. I'm supposed to be cool and I'm anything but right now.

"Ever heard of Photoshop, Jayd?" Jeremy asks, almost snickering in my face. Now he's just being a smart-ass and I don't appreciate it one bit.

"He's right, Jayd," Chance says, now adding to the denial mix. "Anything can be altered nowadays with the right program and skills. Let me see the picture again. I'm going to send it to my phone and see what I can find out."

Nigel steps on the porch and walks over to me for support even if I know he's inclined to agree with his boys.

I hand Chance my cell, and he quickly retrieves the photo and sends it to his iPhone. He's good when it comes to technology, unlike me, who still hasn't mastered any of it, including all the bells and whistles of my phone. It would've taken me at least five minutes to do what he just did.

"Whatever, Chance. It still doesn't change the facts, no matter what you think you can come up with."

"Jayd, you know me," Jeremy says, taking my left hand in

his and pleading with his eyes, but I'm over it. "I'd never do anything to intentionally hurt you, and you should know by now that I'd never cheat on you."

Before I can get sucked up into his pretty blues, Mickey pulls in the driveway with a packed car and I'm grateful for the intrusion.

"Yeah, and I know you're a man, too. I thought I could trust you, Jeremy, but now I don't know what to think." I refuse to cry in front of him, but tears are welling up in my eyes despite my best efforts to be hard.

"I love you, Jayd. Remember that." Finally defeated, Jeremy lets go and says his good-byes before returning to Chance's ride.

Rah emerges from inside the house to help with the final load. "Y'all leaving without helping?" Rah looks ready to cuss them both out, but luckily he's too mellow to go that far.

Chance looks remorseful that he can't stay longer, but under the circumstances he doesn't have much of a choice. "Yeah, man. I got your back later, Nigel. Let me get my man home real quick."

Nigel nods his head affirmatively and shoots Rah a look that says to let it go. Nigel then looks at Mickey's packed car and shakes his head before going inside to make more room for her stuff. Good luck.

"What did I miss?" Rah, who's feeling out of the loop and overworked can't let it slide—not with another full car to unpack.

"I better check on the girls," I say, avoiding Rah's question while listening through the baby monitor attached to my waist. I put them both down for a nap about an hour ago, even though Rahima was resistant to the idea. She'll be three at the end of the month and now that she's not the baby of the crew anymore, feels she's also too old to sleep with

Nickey. I wave to Chance and glare hard at Jeremy before joining Nigel inside.

I peak into Rah's little brother Kamal's room and check on the girls, who look settled in their sleep for the time being. Soon it'll be dinnertime for everyone and I have to be in the house before nightfall—Mama's orders.

"Hey, y'all," Mickey says, entering the living room with a strange look on her face and no bags in hand. "Nigel, Rah needs you outside."

"All right," Nigel says, leaving us alone in the room. He takes one more look at the overstuffed living room, sighs deeply, and steps back outside to finish the task at hand.

"Jayd, I need your help," Mickey whispers, reaching into her skirt pocket and handing me a folded envelope. "My ex-man knows about Tre and me."

This can't be good. I open the letter to see Mickey's incarcerated ex-boyfriend's handwriting in red ink and read the words aloud.

"And the woman was arrayed in purple and scarlet color, and decked with gold and precious stones and pearls, having a golden cup in her hand full of abominations and filthiness of her fornication. Revelations, 17:4." At least he's making good use of his time reading, like most brothers who are locked up.

The biblical words are repeated over and over again on each line of the ruled page. The epic tale of the whore of Babylon looks like blood spilled across the page and I know it has more to do with than his gang allegiance. It gives me chills just touching the page.

Mickey looks nervously toward the front door and I don't blame her. If Nigel sees this he's going to go ballistic, which is exactly why she should tell him before he finds out some other way about her unwanted pen pal.

"Are you going to tell Nigel?" I ask, refolding the letter and slipping it back into the white envelope. I know Mickey thought she was saved when her ex-man was arrested, but far from it. If anyone's too hood for his own good, it's Mickey's former man. We don't have to see his spinning chrome wheels creep around the streets of Compton for the time being like the predator that he is, but we all know his penitentiary address is just temporary. No matter the charge, he always makes his way back to the hood.

"No, and you can't say a word to anyone. I need your help, Jayd," Mickey says, alluding to my spiritual powers.

It always trips me out how my friends and enemies alike will come to me for my spiritual assistance when they're desperate, but judge me every other day of the week for practicing voodoo. It wasn't too long ago Mickey was pissed that I used my mom's gift of sight to absorb her labor pains. Now she's begging for more of my healing. Go figure.

"This is serious, Mickey." I look toward the girls' room already scared for their safety if Mickey's ex finds out where they live. Who knows what he's bound to do if he finds out that she and Nigel are living together with Tre's baby. The shit will hit the fan and go flying all over the neighborhood.

"I know. That's why I need you to handle it for me, Jayd, please. My ex needs to go away—forever." Mickey's eyes are more intense than I've ever seen before, almost scaring me she's so frightened.

"I'll see what I can do." My friend and I lock eyes feeling the depth of the pact we've just made. I'll do whatever I can to keep my family safe and that includes my crew.

Nickey Shantae screams out of her nap and I know she heard everything her mother and I just said. I know how Mickey feels. I want my enemies to disappear, too. Payback's a bitch, or two in my case with Sandy and Cameron tripping hard. But for Mickey and her ex-thug-of-man, it's downright dangerous. Bristol Palin makes being a teenaged mother seem glamorous and dealing with her ex-boyfriend easy-breezy Cover Girl, but that's far from the reality. As Mickey's learning the hard way, all that glitters is definitely not gold or any other kind of metal. All that's shining over here is bull and she's ass-deep in it.

~ 2 ~

Sittin' on Chrome

You sold your soul to the evil and the lust
And the passion and the money?"

—NNEKA

What a week it's already been and it's only Monday. Mama and Netta are busy at the beauty shop and I've been working in the spirit room at Mama's house in Compton all day, as usual. I never knew there was so much involved in being a newly initiated priestess. Instead of cleaning out the vessels and other various items on our family shrines once a week, I have to clean them daily and they each have their own specific rituals. And now with my own vessels to care for it means more work for me. But if it's one thing I know how to do it's how to get my hustle on and that includes my spirit work, too.

According to the spirit book, I can recite an odu—story of one my ancestors including the orisha—and use it to fall into a sort of trance and claim the sight used within the moral tale to get through whatever situation I may be dealing with. So basically, all this time I've been dreaming about the paths of the women who came before me and sometimes retaining their powers I should instead be able to do that through controlled daydreaming. When I master that skill I'll be the baddest chick ever.

While studying my own assignments I'm also researching the Bible verse Mickey got in the mail Saturday. I'll have to get the letter from Mickey next time I see her to search for more clues about her ex-man's next move. With his cryptic ass we never know what's going to happen next. Something's off about the verse he chose and I have a feeling this is just the tip of his vengeful iceberg.

If Mama caught me off my game she'd be disappointed, especially with all of the laundry and other chores I've got in front of me. Constantly wearing white isn't easy, and as soon as anything I'm wearing gets dirty I have to change, thus the never-ending loads.

"Hey, Tweet," Daddy says, walking into the living room where I've set up shop. My uncles are out in the streets and Jay is hanging at his friend's house. Until my grandfather came home, I was the only one here and loving it.

"Hey, Daddy," I say, closing the Bible before rising from the dining room table to give him a kiss on the cheek. I walk over to the couch and sit down ready to work. It's only seven and if I get through this basket quickly I can take a bath before everyone else gets home. I'll be so glad to get back to my mom's apartment in a couple of weeks. I wish I could snap my fingers and make it happen sooner. Even with my jerk of an uncle Karl gone, it's still too many people in this house for me.

"What are you reading?" Daddy eyes the weathered Bible Mama gave me when I was christened as a baby. I remember the day vaguely, but when I touch the worn, white Bible it feels like it was yesterday. As a caul baby, Nickey Shantae should be able to recall some of her earliest moments when she's older, too.

"Oh, I was just looking over a verse I came across for more clarification."

Daddy looks up from the Bible and smiles like a kid in a candy store. I return the smile and continue to fold my fresh whites praying the conversation's over. I just want to get on with my evening and chill for a while before Mama gets home. I know once she walks in I'll have something else to do.

"You know, Jayd, the new youth pastor at the church is overwhelmed with all of the students enrolled. He needs help teaching the last week of vacation Bible school," Daddy says matter-of-factly tapping the leather-bound cover before zipping it closed for me. Why is he telling me about his church business? Daddy has to know I'm not the one to teach the Bible to anyone.

"I'm sorry to hear that," I say. Daddy continues tapping my small Bible, reminding me of when we would go to see Daddy preach every Sunday. I used to love dressing up in my Sunday best and pretending that the clutch-sized Holy Book was a purse. I wanted to be just like Mama and still do in a lot of ways.

"Well, Tweet, you shouldn't be. The job's yours if you want it. Your grandmother told me you couldn't work on anyone's hair until you're given the okay, but teaching is still allowed. It pays ten dollars an hour. Think about it and let me know."

Damn, that's some nice change for back to school clothes. When I was initiated, Mama's clients showered both her and I with lots of gifts. Most of them had cash attached, but it isn't enough to make up for the money I'm missing not working.

"What's the catch?"

Daddy watches me fold my lapas, headscarves, and other white clothes blinded by the seemingly endless wave of white. I know how he feels. I can't wait to throw a splash of color in the mix.

"The catch is you get to do something good for four days and get paid well while doing it. I'll talk to your grandmother about it, but I'm sure it'll be okay with her. Even iyawos can work in the church." Daddy winks at me as both our cells ring. From the wide smile across his face I know it's not Mama. Daddy walks toward the front door and out to his clean Cadillac parked in the driveway. Even the chrome wheels are shining in the evening sun. Daddy's going out and as usual it's without his wife. Can men ever be trusted?

"What up, Nigel?" I say, flipping my phone open and wedging it between my left shoulder and ear. I can't afford to lose another minute of folding if I want to get in the bathroom while I still have some privacy.

"What up, chick? You coming over Rah's tonight? Chance wants to holler at you about something and he asked me to give you a call since he and his mom are at the movies right now."

I'm so glad Chance forgave his mom and they're back to their old ways. I know they still have a lot of healing to do with her hiding his adoption all these years, but they love each other and will make it through this crisis. It also helps that I put a little something on the two of them to help with their hot heads. With a little patience and understanding Chance and Mrs. Carmichael moved toward forgiveness by themselves.

"Nah, bro. I can't make it this evening, but I'll try and catch y'all tomorrow after work." Usually I would turn down a job teaching at Daddy's church, but it's only four days and I need the money.

"Bet. By the way, Chance wanted to let you know he's still looking into the photograph and that he spoke to Cameron. The trick admits she straddled Jeremy in the chair and kissed him. Chance also suspects that even if the picture's real, she set up the whole thing to look like more than it was."

I know I should feel some sense of relief, but I don't. All I feel is sick to my stomach at the thought of that heffa touching my man.

"What does she weigh, like a buck ten? Jeremy could've

kept her off his lap if he really wanted to." I'm not giving an inch on the matter. "No matter how it happened, the facts remain the same. They were kissing and had the audacity to make a permanent record of the shit." My laundry's taking the brunt of my frustration. I'm just glad it's not one of my clients' heads.

"Jayd, sometimes you're too hood for your own good, you know that?" Nigel says, half laughing. I know he's not calling me hood when he and his baby mama are shacking up with his best friend. If that's not hood then I don't know what is.

"What's that supposed to mean?" I ask, folding my clothes harder than necessary. I was cool until this phone call. Now I'm getting hot all over again and that's the last thing I need.

"It means sometimes you're too damn hard on a nigga, Jayd." Nigel sighs heavily and I can feel his frustration. "Jeremy didn't mean any harm and Cameron admits to being the one who kissed him, not the other way around. I thought you'd be happy knowing the truth."

"Nigel, where have we heard this story before?" If this doesn't sound like Rah and Sandy's twisted love story my name's not Jayd Jackson.

"I know what it sounds like and I'm not the one to defend Jeremy, but he's not Rah." He sounds just like Jeremy now, always claiming he and my ex-boyfriend are nothing alike.

Rah's never cared for me dating Jeremy for many reasons, the main one being that Rah will always have a soft spot for me. And Jeremy doesn't like it that Rah and me share a special connection that baffles him. They both have more in common than they realize. Maybe they'll be great friends once I'm not dating either of them.

"I'm just too real for that shit, Nigel, and you know it."

I stack the last of the towels in the wicker basket and head to Mama's room to put them up. There's still no drawer or closet space for me in this house, so my clean laundry stays in the basket and the dirty laundry goes in another one at the foot of my twin bed across from my grandmother's matching bed. It's been nice being back with Mama. I need her and she needs me, but I think even she has to admit I've outgrown this space in more ways than one.

"Yes, Jayd. We all know you like to keep it one hundred and all, but this time keeping it real might be the wrong way to go. It's just a suggestion, girl. You know I've got your back either way."

Maybe Nigel and Chance are right. I can give Jeremy a pass this time. After all, I did kiss Mr. Adewale, even if I was in a trance and thought we were my great-grandparents at the time. Luckily the shit happened off school property and it's our little secret, saving us both the embarrassment and Mr. Adewale his job. But Cameron's not getting off so easy. She hasn't encountered anyone from my hood being crossed and I'm going to make sure she never does it again. The only way to stop chicks like her is to give them a taste of their own medicine and that's just what I intend to do. Quitting Jeremy would be playing into her hand and this is one game she'd better be prepared to lose.

"I'll talk to Jeremy, but I just can't put my feelings into words—not yet." Until then I have nothing to say to my estranged boyfriend. I knew him leaving for six weeks was too long to remain faithful. Hell, I almost wasn't my damn self and I didn't leave Southern California this summer.

"It's a long time for anyone to be faithful, especially a teenaged boy, Jayd," my mom says, all up in the mix. *"It's a bit ridiculous for either one of y'all to be committed solely to each other your senior year of high school anyway, if you ask me."*

"Mom, weren't you engaged to my dad by then?" I ask, eyeing my white-on-white ensemble for tomorrow. I might as well pick out my work clothes so I won't have to do it in the

morning. Just because I have to wear one color doesn't mean I still can't put my individual stamp on it. I've started tying my head wrap in the front like the tignon my great-grandmother used to wear in New Orleans. Mama says it's just like a child of Oshune to want to shine even when she's supposed to be at her most humble.

"My point exactly, smart-ass. Think about it and I'll check in with you later. My boss is talking to me and I guess I should listen to some of his crap so I can get out of here and go home." My mom is so funny sometimes. I guess she has a hard time focusing on two conversations at once much like I do whenever she jumps in my head.

"All right, Jayd. I'll holla," Nigel says, almost ending the call, but not before Mickey overhears the last part of our conversation.

"Nigel, is that Jayd on the phone?" I hear Mickey ask in the background. I know she wants to grill me about what I'm doing in regards to her ode to a harlot, but I'm not in the mood.

"Mickey wants to holla at you real quick, Queen." Nigel's so sweet. Mickey would probably go crazy if she ever lost him. There would be a line down the block if word got out that Nigel was single with Nellie right at the front. No matter who she's dating now, if Nigel ever got loose from Mickey's iron grip she'd jump at the chance to date him.

"We're going shopping at the swap meet tomorrow afternoon. Can you make it or what?" Mickey asks. She sounds annoyed, but I'm not going to get into it with her now about what's up her butt this evening. My goal is to get off this phone as soon as possible.

"Yeah, I guess so. I get off work at one. I'll meet y'all there." I spot a bottle of lavender bath salts and claim it for my running water.

"And bring your money, Jayd. I'll be damned if you're

wearing all white on your first day of school. If you do that the whole year will start off bad."

"Whatever, Mickey. And you bring the letter. I need to inspect it further."

I got an idea on how to jump into the mind of the author through the strokes of a person's handwriting. Maman Marie was excellent with her skills. She could study her clients' writing and tell whether or not they were honest people. I want to try something similar with Mickey's letter. There's a reason he wrote the words the way he did and in the color of blood. I just hope I can figure out his plan before he does harm to my girls or my boy.

"Okay, Jayd. Bye."

"Good night, Mickey."

Finally, the quiet before the storm. Mama should be home by eight giving me a half hour to myself. Once my four uncles, my cousin Jay, and my grandmother filter in from their separate days all bets are off when it comes to peace in this small house. I can always escape to the spirit room when need be and tonight will probably be one of those times. I'm going to need all the help I can get to teach young kids for the rest of the week without snapping. Lord knows I barely have the patience to deal with my teenaged friends. But money is money and as long as they keep it cool, so will I.

After my bath last night, I had just enough time to myself to cover my body in Mama's lemon and coconut oil blend and eat dinner before the procession of my family members began. By the time Mama was done at the shop I was camped out in the back house, reading my spirit notes and trying to master the new things I've learned over the past few weeks. Sad to say, but I don't miss cheer at all nor am I looking forward to returning to the squad next week. The practice and game schedule will continue to mess up my cheddar and I'm not feeling losing any more money. I'm glad the last four days of this week will be spent making money, I've missed my financial independence.

I pull up to the quaint church house and park in a space up front. The driveway is longer than the actual building. I could've walked from Mama's house to Daddy's church up the block, but it's too hot to be outside any longer than necessary.

The alarm on my phone rings loudly in the compact car, reminding me to put it on vibrate before I walk inside. I scheduled my new gig into the calendar just to see if the thing really works. Ever since Chance played with my phone the other day I've started to explore its features.

The first thing I notice when I step into the bright space is the loud noise level so early in the morning. There are children ranging from four years old to eleven everywhere, talking loudly and running around like chickens with their heads cut off. I knew there was a catch. I have to work with kids straight out of hell.

"Jayd, it's nice to see you again." A nicely dressed young brotha comes up to me with his right hand extended as if students aren't wreaking havoc all around the front meeting hall. What have I gotten myself into and how can I get out?

"Again?" I don't remember the first time we met and I wouldn't forget this brotha. He's almost as short as I am and although he has a nice smile, his foul breath makes me want to indefinitely hold mine.

"I didn't have the opportunity to officially introduce myself after your eloquent speech on Easter Sunday. I'm Wendell Godfry, youth pastor."

"It's nice to meet you, sir." I return the gesture while simultaneously attempting to breathe over my right shoulder, but there's no escaping this dude's halitosis. Maybe the kids are acting bad because they can't take his breath anymore. I know I want to run away.

"There'll be none of that 'sir' stuff, girl. We aren't that far apart in age. When your grandfather told me you'd be relieving Mrs. Pratt for the rest of the week I felt like the heavens opened up and answered my prayers."

"Is that so?" I ask, trying not to be too obvious while diverting my nose away from his mouth. I walk into the eye of the storm where ten of the twenty or so students are playing dodge ball in the middle of the room. Really? I know they're kids but there's no order in here at all. When I attended vacation Bible school it was nothing like this.

"Yes, it was—not that I wanted Mrs. Pratt gone, but her pressure couldn't take these active whippersnappers another day," Wendell says, looking at the kids as if the mischief they're causing is normal. He obviously has little experience with children and they know it.

"Where do I start?" I ask, scared to put my purse down for fear I'll never see it again.

Wendell points toward the double doors leading to the main sanctuary. On either side of the doors are two portable white boards with markers and erasers accompanying both. He leads me through the crowd who suddenly becomes interested about the new person in the room.

"Why are you dressed like that?" a boy who looks to be about seven or eight asks as I approach the far end of the hall to help round everyone up for our morning salutation.

"Yeah, you a Muslim or something?" another young boy asks, holding the dodge ball. "My daddy says I can't talk to y'all." I don't care what his daddy says, all I know is that if he hits me with that ball he's going to pray to whatever God he can that I don't catch him.

I glare at both curious boys and continue my trek. I'll address all questions after I introduce myself. Finally at the double doors, I take a marker and write my name across the board while Wendell calls everyone to attention. I see why Daddy wanted me here—Miss Jayd doesn't take any mess and they're all about to find out.

"We have a new teacher with us this morning, hallelujah!" Wendell exclaims, scaring several girls in the now seated group. The three long tables each seat ten, with a few seats empty to spare. With only two teachers to pay, the church must be making a nice piece of change from the summer program. From previous experience I know most of the tuitions are paid by state funds for the children on public assistance. The others are privately sponsored by nonprofit organizations. Daddy's got a good thing going on here while helping out the neighborhood.

"Hi. My name is Miss Jayd and I'm going to be with y'all for the rest of the week."

At first glance, the kids look like they've seen a ghost. They can't stop staring at me and I can see the millions of questions running through their minds.

"I'll address the elephant in the room once and for all, then we have to get on with our morning."

"I don't see no elephant," a pretty, brown-skinned girl says, her ponytails completely uneven. If I could get in that head I would braid her thick, black hair in a pretty style to hug her round face. "Are you a nurse or something?" she asks, breaking the silence for the other students to ask the first thing that comes to mind.

"Okay, settle down," Wendell says. The kids completely ignore him, as they should. No one can hear his soft voice over these loud children.

"Ago," I call loudly. This is how my elders call in Yoruba to get our attention and it always works.

The students look at me even more strangely as I repeat the word.

"When I say 'ago,' which means 'are you there,' y'all say 'beni,' which means 'yes.' Let's try it again. Ago," I call, this time with a smile. Maybe they're not so unruly after all.

"Beni," they say in unison, some giggling at the strange words lingering in the air. Wendell looks at me in amazement. I wonder how long it usually takes him to gain order when I'm not here, if he ever does.

"Very good. When I said the elephant, I was talking about my very bright attire."

A few of the children snicker to one another while the others look on ready for my story.

"Very quickly, I am in training, a religious training, so to speak. Soon I will be able to wear jeans and colorful clothing again, but right now I have to wear white to symbolize my commitment to my way of life."

"Okay, thank you for that introduction, Miss Jayd. Would you mind erasing that board while I begin this morning's class?" Wendell points to the board with my name on it and takes control of the class. I guess he doesn't want me talking too much about voodoo in the house of the Lord, just like Daddy.

"Young people, are we ready to study the three r's: reading, writin', and religion?" Wendell asks, putting his hands up in the air like he's cheering.

No he did not just say that. Where's this dude from and why is he in Compton? The kids and I all look at him like the fool he's portraying himself to be.

"So, how are we doing up here?" Daddy asks, coming up the stairs from his office just in time to save his youth pastor from any further embarrassment. I saw him this morning before I left. He must've arrived a few minutes after I did.

"Oh, just fine, Pastor James. I was introducing everyone to Miss James here and we're about ready for the lady of the house to jump in where she sees fit." He's really on some

Southern shit for real. Wendell steps closer to me and puts his left arm around my shoulders, forcing me to put my face in his forearm.

"Excellent. That's what I like to see." Daddy smiles and smacks his left hand hard with the folded papers in his right hand. The look in his eyes tells me this was all a well orchestrated setup. Did he really think I'd be interested in this cat? If so, my grandfather doesn't know me at all.

"It's Jackson. My last name is Jackson," I say, removing Wendell's arm and sitting down at the middle table, facing the class. I want to say more, but I'm supposed to keep a cool head and Daddy's in the room making me check myself even more.

"Please forgive me. Miss Jackson," Wendell says, smiling big and bright, much to Daddy's liking. This is too much.

"Pastor James, the Women's Guild is ready for you," a woman's voice says. I bet they are.

One of the church ladies who hates the thought of Mama comes up the stairs behind Daddy and stares me down. I wish she would say something cross to me. I remember her as one of the hackling hens from Easter service. She had rude things to say about both my mom and my grandmother. If she steps my way I'll have to give her a taste of her own medicine.

"Well, you two carry on," Daddy says, feeling the pressure from behind. Why do these women have so much power over my grandfather and why do they feel they can boss another woman's husband around? "I'm sure this will be the most productive week yet. And Jayd, don't be afraid to take some initiative. We men need a little help even when we're too proud to ask."

"Yes, sir," Wendell says in true kiss-ass style. He wants to be just like Pastor James when he grows up.

Daddy waves to us before ducking back downstairs where

his fan club awaits. I know my granddaddy's got the whole "pimping ain't easy" swag down, but he doesn't take the shit seriously or at least I thought he didn't. I can't believe Daddy's trying to pimp me out to his little protégé. As if. That may be the name of the car I drive, but it ain't me at all. I'll talk to him about this later at home. I'm sure Daddy thinks it would be a match made in heaven or somewhere very close to it, but it ain't happening. Suddenly I can't wait until this day is over. I'll tell my girls all about Reverend Funky Breath and my grandfather's failed attempt to marry me off to him at the swap meet this afternoon. Until then, I have to work for my money. If today was a prelude to my temporary job description, this is going to be a really long week.

~ 3 ~
Golden Child

Hard to move on when you always regret one.

—Miguel featuring J. Cole

I thought Wendell would never let me go once the children were dismissed for the day. He convinced me to stay an extra hour to help prepare their art projects for tomorrow's assignment, throwing in the fact that we get paid for an extra hour of prep time every day. I couldn't pass up the money and won't for the rest of the week, even if that means I have to listen to Wendell talk about being a virtuous young woman for the entire sixty minutes. Much like himself, he sees me as a golden child of sorts—chosen by God and Pastor James to do the Lord's work. I wish Mama was there to set his ass straighter than a flat iron on pressed hair.

One thing that stuck out from our conversation was Wendell quoting the Bible, the book of Revelations in particular. I questioned Wendell about the whore of Babylon verses and he jumped at the chance to show off his biblical knowledge while inadvertently bringing some clarity to the reading for me. If I understand correctly, the whore is actually a metaphor for one of several abominations before the end of the world. Like I said before, I know Mickey's ex is planning something and if this is just the beginning, whatever it is must be catastrophic. I need to get that letter from Mickey. I hope she remembers to bring it.

* * *

Almost every car in the packed lot outside the Compton Fashion Center, a.k.a the swap meet, has rims, except for mine and maybe five others. What really gets me are the old, run-down cars with shiny chrome wheels worth more than the vehicle itself. There's even a rent-a-rim shop outside the swap meet for people who don't have the money to buy the expensive tire gear outright. Only in the hood would you see some shit like this.

When I walk into the bustling swap meet all eyes are on me—the girl in all white. I feel like I'm on display, but it comes with the territory. I send my girls a quick text to find out where they are. The quicker I have my folks around me, the better. There's safety in numbers and flying solo is anything but.

Even if Mama's allowing me to come out of whites for the school year—even if tradition mandates an iyawo should wear white for an entire year—she's not letting up on my undergarments and the fact that I have to wear white when I'm in the shop and the spirit room. She made it clear that I need all new white underwear to wear for the next three months—no exceptions. I'm just grateful she's being lenient when it comes to school. The last thing I need is sticking out unnecessarily on the first day.

The underwear in the large flea market are nothing like the ones at Victoria's Secret. When Jeremy took me on my shopping spree for my birthday, it was the first time I'd ever splurged on the expensive bras and panties. I wish I could wear them now, but the ones from Target I have on will have to do. They're not bad, but a sistah like me with a full D cup size needs all the support I can get.

"What up, Mother Teresa?" Mickey says as she and Nellie round the corner ahead of me. That's her new nickname for me while I'm in whites and I don't mind. It could be worse, so I'll take it as the love it's meant to be.

"I love it," Nellie says, the first to hug me and I return the gesture. "I think it's chic, like LisaRaye McCoy." Nellie's so silly sometimes, but I know she means well. Why she chooses her role models is a whole other issue.

"What up, y'all? Where's the baby?" I ask, missing the presence of our newest crewmember, Nickey. New life changes everything and my crew's no exception. It feels good having Nickey's sweet presence around and it's a good reminder to use birth control for my sexually active friends. Mama's all the reminder I need to stay a virgin until I'm ready to deal with all of the consequences that come with giving it up too soon.

"At home with her daddy," Mickey says, giving me a quick hug while slyly passing the letter. It's best for Nellie to stay out of the loop on this one for the time being. The girl can barely hold water let alone something this huge. "She was napping when I left and Lord knows I didn't want to wake her."

Smart girl. Mickey's motherly instincts are finally kicking in, thanks in part to Dr. Whitmore's special postnatal blend of herbs. I finally told Mickey I switched the pills Misty gave her via Esmeralda with the healthy ones from Dr. Whitmore so she'd continue taking them. The last thing we need is for Mickey to have another meltdown. She was irritated at first, but Mickey has learned to live with it and she's better off for it. I think both my girls are finally learning to trust my gifts as the blessings they are. I've had a hard time dealing with the crazy dreams and other visions that come with my growing powers, but they're a part of me just like everything else I was born with. My powers aren't going anywhere so we'd all better get used to having a priestess in the crew.

"How are y'all adjusting to the move?" I ask. We continue walking up the tight paths of clothing, household items, and baby crap everywhere the eye can see. It's amazing we can find anything in this place.

"It's actually the best thing for our little family," Mickey says, eyeing the glass-enclosed gold jewelry along the aisles. "Nigel and me have more time together and the baby sleeps through the night now that we can close the door and chill in the living room. Not to mention we have our own bathroom. I love it."

I'm sure Mickey does because it's a step up for her. But I know Nigel's having a hard time leaving his mini mansion where he had his own floor and all the amenities of a retired NBA player's only son. I wouldn't be surprised if he's seriously doubting his decision to move out of his parents' house, but love will make us all do some crazy things.

"How's Jeremy?" Nellie asks, bringing up the thorn in my side. Why did she have to go there, and on such a pleasant afternoon, too?

"I don't know. I haven't talked to him since his pop-up visit over the weekend." I take stock of the packs of white socks and underwear in one section to compare it to the multiple others I'll run into by the time it's all said and done. There's no point in paying full price at the swap meet when everything's negotiable.

My girls look at me and then at each other before rolling their eyes. I look around knowing that heat wasn't for me.

"What was that all about?" I know these heffas don't have anything to say about my relationship status.

Neither Mickey nor Nellie are experts when it comes to love. Nellie chose some punk she met at church over Chance, and Mickey's in no position to give anyone advice about relationships, especially not when it comes to cheating. She wrote the book on lying to your partner and getting away with it.

"You're tripping, that's what," Mickey says, stopping at one of the many jewelry counters in the sprawling place. She eyes wedding sets wishing Nigel would buy her a bigger ring and make it official. I say Mickey better learn to count her blessings and slow her roll. The fact she and Nigel are living together is a miracle in and of itself. She needs to be happy with the dainty diamondlike promise ring she's got and call it a day. Nigel's an exceptional dude to claim another man's baby and stick it out with Mickey's high maintenance ass.

"How is it that my boyfriend's the cheater and I'm the one being persecuted?" Really? This is how it's going to be. I thought at least my girls would hold my grudge with me.

"He didn't cheat on you, Jayd. Damn, lighten up." Mickey sucks her teeth in disgust.

"It was just a kiss," Nellie says, also eyeing the jewelry inside the case. The Chinese saleswoman behind the counter gestures toward the earrings, rings, and various necklaces and charms to see if my girls want to try anything on. They both shake their heads and continue daydreaming. These days we're all strapped for cash.

Mickey's got a skewed view of loyalty within relationships so I know she thinks she's being reasonable. But Nellie's much more conservative with her views. I'm surprised by her forgiving attitude. I guess it's from all the churching she's been doing lately. Maybe I should introduce her to Pastor Halitosis. They might hit it off and Nellie may be just the girl to improve his style—bad breath and all.

"Nellie, if Jeremy was your boyfriend would you be so forgiving? All Chance did was leave for the summer and you didn't show him any love."

Nellie slits her dark, brown eyes at me, flipping her blond-streaked weave over her right shoulder. I'll be so grateful when she gets off of this blond kick. At least it's not completely blond like it was before she got her tracks tightened last week. That was too much for all of us to bare, including Chance.

"That was totally different, Jayd." Nellie is living on an island of denial all by herself. "Besides, everything is not what it seems. You don't know what really happened between Jeremy and Cameron."

Something about Nellie's guarded answer tells me she knows more about the situation than she's letting on. Cameron's an extended member of the rich bitch crew Nellie's been trying so desperately to hold on to. But when she gives up her Homecoming crown next month she'll officially turn in her membership card to that crew along with it. Unless she wins Homecoming princess or queen this year her days of hanging with Laura, Tania, and the rest of their wannabes are in the past and I for one am glad for it.

"I agree with Nellie. What you need to do is check that trick as soon as you see her perky, white ass Monday. I bet she'll confess the whole truth and nothing but the truth if you step to her correctly."

"That's not what I said," Nellie says with a mortified look on her face. What's she so afraid of? She knows how Mickey is—when all else fails, our girl goes straight for the jugular.

"Mickey, I'm not trying to fight anyone on the first day of school. That's all I need to start my year off on the wrong foot again." Bad memories of my first day back to South Bay High last year come to the front of my mind. I didn't even make it off the bus before this chick, Trecee, fronted me about KJ's trifling ass because of some shit Misty started. I'm so happy I have my mom's car to roll I don't know what to do.

"Jayd, are you getting soft on me, girl?" Mickey says, playfully punching me in my left shoulder. "Where's the Compton at, girl?" Mickey's so stupid.

"It's right here, chick," I say, returning the soft punch. "Don't get it twisted because I want to graduate this year." I've never had to fight Mickey and wouldn't want to go there. Between the two of us, I think I'd eventually wear Mickey's ass down, but it would be an even match making for an ugly battle no one wants to witness, least of all me.

Nellie shakes her head and smiles at us. We do make quite the trio. The other customers look at us and keep moving. As long as there's no gun involved nobody really gives a damn what we do, as long as we spend money while doing it.

"Speaking of celebrations, what are we doing for my birthday?" Mickey asks, flipping through the various racks of knockoff designer jeans. Nellie turns up her nose at the illegal apparel, but her eyes brighten when she notices the imitation Gucci bags across the way. There's something for everyone at the Compton Fashion Center.

"You mean *our* birthday," Nellie says, rolling her eyes at our girl before checking out the pretty bags.

My girls are a mess. It's Mama's birthday I'm more concerned with. It's this Sunday with Labor Day right after, and then the first day of school. Usually Mama, Netta, and I would spend the day shopping and eating, maybe even catching a movie. Mickey and Nellie's birthdays are later in the month and a week apart. Usually they celebrate separately, which has always served me well. That way I can focus all of my attention on Mama and not have to deal with my girls competing for everyone's attention, including mine.

"Fine, whatever. Our birthdays. Are we going to dinner, throwing a party or what?" Mickey picks out a size four jeans and a shirt to match. She's looking more and more like her pre-baby self and feeling like it, too.

"Oooh, we should throw a dinner party at Benihana's. Tania's family threw her a beautiful baby shower at the one in Beverly Hills," Nellie says, smelling the fake bag before trying it on. I got my Coach bag from here a couple of years ago and it lasted me well until Jeremy bought the real Lucky bag I've been sporting for the past year.

Mickey and I look at Nellie like she's lost her mind. I feel for my girl being excommunicated from the rich bitch crew, but she has to know it was for the best. Her family may be financially better off than Mickey's and mine, but she's far from rich. The sooner Nellie comes back down to Earth the better.

"Nellie, you're tripping if you think we've got money to spend on some fool flipping knives in the air and starting fires and shit," Mickey says, claiming more clothes for her ever-growing stack.

I couldn't have said it better myself. It's been hard enough trying to conserve what money I have left from a very profitable first half of the summer. I'll be damned if I'm giving up any of it for a show. As a matter of fact, I'll pass on purchasing anything today and wait until I get my check from the church. Besides, I like the selection at Target better. I place my few items down on the counter and endure the evil stare from the salesman who'll reluctantly have to return them to their rightful spot. Oh, well. I have the right to change my mind and I just did.

"Mickey, you're so ghetto sometimes, I swear. You need to expand your horizons." Nellie holds onto her new purse and eyes everything else like it's shit on the bottom of her shoe.

Sometimes? Has Nellie met Mickey? Ain't nothing changed about Mickey except for the fact she's a mother now. Aside from that our girl's as real as ever with the acrylic claws to prove it.

"I'll expand them by adding shrimp to the menu. How's that?" Mickey counts her loot and looks around to see if there's anything she missed before paying for it. She's got enough clothes to last her the entire year, but I know this is only her wardrobe for the first two weeks. Mickey wouldn't be caught dead in the same outfit twice within the first month of school.

Nellie laughs at Mickey and I can't help but to laugh at them both. I agree with Nellie; Mickey should definitely open her mind a bit, but we have to start with baby steps. To throw Mickey into Beverly Hills dining is like throwing a baby lion to a pack of hungry hyenas—the snooty broads on the west side would eat her alive just because they can.

"Okay then. A cocktail party it is." Nellie has to put her boogie touch on it or it's not real to her.

Mickey and I exchange a smile, shake our heads and let our girl have her way with words. They'll only be seventeen, but to Nellie, every birthday is golden.

As Nellie pays for her non-designer bag, Mickey pulls me to the side and I already know what it's about. I don't blame her for not telling Nellie about her pen pal. She did let it slip that Nellie has a new friend in front of Chance a couple of weeks ago, creating more tension than need be before they officially called it quits. Friend or not, it would be just like a broad to pay Mickey back by not-so-accidentally telling Nigel about the letter Mickey's ex-man sent.

"Did you work on ridding me of that nigga's bull?" Mickey whispers. The fear in her eyes is real and I feel for my girl. Her ex-boyfriend is the craziest gangster I know and she's right to be concerned.

"Not yet. Did you tell Nigel?" Even if he would be pissed

as all get-out I still think she should tell him. When in a relationship, keeping secrets is the quickest way to end up single.

"Hell no and I'm not going to. If you handle it for me he'll never need to find out."

When will Mickey ever learn she can't keep covering her tracks? Sooner or later the truth always rears its head and it's never a pretty sight. Before we can get too deep into the conversation an unwelcomed visitor approaches us with all the nerve she's got and then some.

"What's up, bitches?" Misty says, immediately causing Mickey to snap her neck and take a step toward our schoolmate.

I choose to ignore my best friend turned sworn enemy. Other than Esmeralda, Misty's the only person who can make me see red. I'd think Misty would've learned her lesson about messing with Mickey and in public no less, but apparently young dogs can't learn new tricks.

"You're the only bitch I see," Mickey says, speaking for the three of us. Nellie shakes her head knowing it's about to go down. She pulls her new bag out of the plain black plastic bag the saleslady put it in and displays it proudly on her shoulder for all to see. Nellie's secret is safe with me. Mickey, on the other hand, will call her boogie ass out and let everyone know her Gucci bag has never even seen a Gucci store if she gets out of hand.

"Mickey, let's finish our shopping. We have to get back to Nickey before it gets too late," Nellie says in an attempt to diffuse the already tense situation before it gets out of hand.

I look into Misty's bright blue eyes and feel something more than the usual is off about my frenemy who looks satisfied that she's riled us up, smiling at our reaction. Nellie nudges Mickey's left shoulder and she finally moves forward leaving the drama behind, as we all should. Mickey has a daughter to think about and can't afford any more fights even if she would be justified in whipping Misty's ass. She could argue that she's doing a public service for the community by ridding us all of Misty's crap.

"See you heffas next Tuesday," Misty says, walking past me as my girls lead the way to the front of the busy swap meet. "By the way, Jayd. You look lovely in your whites."

"Whatever," I say, rolling my eyes at Misty, who smiles coyly in return. I stop dead in my tracks knowing I didn't just see fangs in this trick's mouth. And not only that, Misty's eyes seem to be glowing on their own.

"You didn't think you were the only iyawo with growing powers, did you?" Misty whispers into my ear as I attempt to pass her by, her eyes growing brighter by the second. Does anyone else notice this shit?

"What the hell?" I say under my breath in total disbelief. Misty's eyes are a luminous blue and her hair is loose around her face and getting thicker. Am I tripping or is this bitch turning into a werewolf before my eyes? I rub my eyes like I just woke up from a nap and look at Misty again who's still showing off her new tricks. Oh, hell no. Something's definitely wrong with me because this can't be possible.

"Get a grip, Jayd. You may be from the almighty Williams Women bloodline, but y'all ain't the only ones who can switch shit up. Remember that." Misty snaps at me like she's taking a bite of rawhide, turns around and walks away leaving me in a state of shock.

"Jayd, are you okay?" Nellie asks, coming back for me. Mickey is slightly ahead of us both, making her way toward the front of the large space.

"Yeah. I guess I'm just seeing things." I hope that's the case, but everything in my body tells me I just encountered some unnatural shit. I need to get home and talk to Mama about Misty's transformation. That shit can't be normal. "I'm going to head out," I say. Chilling with my crew will have to wait. Misty's growing teeth and bright eyes take priority over new gear and gossip any day.

"Jayd, where are you going? I thought you were coming over Rah's house afterwards?" Mickey asks, looking concerned. She just missed the show, but I have a feeling it was only meant for me to see.

"I'll catch up with y'all later. I forgot I had to take care of something before it gets too late. Tell everyone I said hey and kiss Nickey for me."

I hate to admit it, but hell yeah I thought I was the only one out of me, Misty, and Emilio whose powers would be off the chain after our initiations. I don't know much about what Misty can and can't do now that her evil godmother's got her claws deep in my nemesis, but whatever Misty's assumed powers are shouldn't come with fangs of any type—that I know for sure. So what the hell was that all about?

It took me less than the usual ten minutes for me to drive from one side of Compton to the other. All of the men are home, but Mama's nowhere to be found. Apparently she and Netta had some work to do at a client's house and won't be back any time soon. I don't know what to do about what I saw, but I know it was real and not a crazy vision or daydream. I've been sleeping better than ever with my head still wrapped in white like the rest of my body. Hopefully my crazy days are all behind me. After seeing Misty with two extra-sharp teeth I kind of wish my insane visions weren't a thing of the past just yet.

Rather than deal with my grandfather, uncles, and Jay I head to the backyard for some serious spirit time. I lock the dilapidated wooden gate separating the front yard from the back behind me and walk quietly up the driveway. The last thing I want is to engage anyone in conversation. From what I can see across the side gate Esmeralda's house is dark and no one's home. If Esmeralda came outside I don't think I'd be able to deal with her evil ways anymore this evening. All I can think about is Misty's two, long canine teeth exposed through her glossy red lips. The last thing that girl needs is another weapon in her arsenal.

Reaching the back house I open the door and turn the light switch in to the on position instantly illuminating the intimate space. Mama's been busy and she's got the sticky notes to prove it. Large and small pink and yellow squares with Mama's fancy script cover every cabinet in the small kitchen. Some have lists of ingredients; others have a checklist of all the things Mama needs to get done in a day. There's always work to do in Mama's world.

I set my purse down on the kitchen table next to the wounded spirit book and sigh deeply. One of my major projects is to redo the burnt cover of the ancient text since it was partially because of my neglect the book was burned by my crazy uncle Kurtis in the first place. I'm not sure how to tackle rebinding the leather book, but I'll get started by taking it apart while I look for a passage to tell me about my former friend turning into an animal instead of wearing whites for weeks. What kind of head cleansing did Misty receive?

I pull out a stool, take a seat at the tall table, and gently flip through the large book to the section on our family initiations. Much like the oversized Bible in Mama's living room, we keep a record of important events in this family book. As I browse through the section on stories about developing powers after our formal ceremonies, I see a paragraph entitled "The Golden Child," reminding me that I need to holla at my grandfather about his betrothing my hand in marriage to his understudy. I can't wait to tell Mama about my first day working at the church. She'll really get a kick out of Daddy's failed plan.

"Hey, Lexi," I say, greeting Mama's German shepherd who lies across the threshold in her usual protective position. Since borrowing Esmeralda's powers, which allowed me to hear Lexi's old lady–like voice in my thoughts I've got a new respect for the pooch.

The Golden Child is apparently the one who can move in and out of our ancestors' powers, the dream world, and reality at will. This special person also has the ability to see the walking dead who disguise themselves as everyday people such as zombies, vampires, werewolves, and all around shapeshifters. Sounds kind of like my gifts with the exception of seeing the living dead. That's a skill I'm not sure I want to acquire.

"Don't sell yourself short, Jayd. You don't know what the Creator has in store for you."

My mom always has a way of chiming in at the right time. I glance at the pictures of the Golden Child with luminescent eyes greener than any of the eyes present in our lineage thus far. Maman was a great artist, unlike Mama and I who do our best to paint vivid pictures with words rather than drawings. If I attempted to sketch a thought it would look worse than one of Rahima's stick figures.

"Mom, I'm very happy with my gifts so far. I think seeing dead people walking around would be a bit much," I think back while taking in part of the parable.

Apparently this kid can commune with the dead because, as a child of Oya—the orisha over the wind, graveyards, and transformation of any kind—she blessed this special child with the ability to also send the dead back to the other side, therefore protecting the living from premature death by becoming a mule or zombie as we call them. Mama told me stories of zombies and vampires when I was a child, but I thought they were just that—stories, not something real that would invade one of the biggest haters in my life. Like Misty needs more drama than she already brings on a regular basis.

"Maybe, maybe not. The point is to go with the flow. Falling to sleep and waking up with someone else's powers would trip me out. But if it was there when I woke up what am I going to do, give it back? I don't think so, little sistah."

"Point taken, Mom," I say as she leaves me to my studying. My mom thinks she's slick using my gift of sight as an analogy to this new power not yet born, but I hear her loud and clear.

When my dreams began to evolve—first through sleepwalking, then through keeping the powers I dreamt about once I was awake—it scared the shit out of me. Now that they've matured more I see the value in them. Whatever I saw in Misty today was disturbing, but what if it was a blessing in disguise? Exactly what kind of blessing is a topic for another time. I just want to find out what she's evolving into and how to stop it before it gets out of hand.

"I've got love all over me," Monica sings, announcing a phone call from who I don't know. Mama's the only one with a personal ringtone these days. Against my better judgment I answer the call only because it's from Nellie. I should let it go to voice mail and continue with my reading, but she's probably just checking on me since I abruptly left our shopping spree this afternoon.

"Hello," I answer, still skimming through the spirit book. I don't want to lose my place in the massive text.

"Jayd, you need to get over here right now," Nellie says, frantically interrupting my solitude. I knew I shouldn't have answered the phone.

"What's wrong, and where is 'here'?" I ask, vaguely concerned. My girl has a history of being melodramatic so it's hard to know when to take her seriously.

"At Rah's house. Sandy's here with her new maybe baby daddy and his sister, Trish. It's not a good look, Jayd. Her and Rah are one step away from being on *Jerry Springer*."

"Nellie, they could have been on *Springer* ten times by now," I say, putting the speakerphone on while I thumb through the book. My days of running to Rah's rescue over Sandy are a thing of the past. As one of Rah's best friends I've more than done my job dealing with that crazy broad. But I am interested to know why Rah's supplier and the alleged father of the mystery baby are there with Rah's ex-trick, Trish no less. I'm sure she jumped at the excuse to visit Rah. That girl's so sprung it's unattractive.

"Jayd, save the sarcasm. This is serious and Mickey's not here to handle Sandy's irrational behavior. She went to get her nails done while I watch Nickey. I don't know what to do."

Mickey needs to fill out some job applications instead of spending money she doesn't have. Between her hair and nails Mickey could easily skim at least two hundred off her monthly bills. That alone would help out her little family. She doesn't know it yet but Rah's going to start laying down the law, including who does what chores and who's responsible for which bills. He's the most responsible seventeen-year-old dude I've ever known. He and Nigel will be eighteen next month and I know they'll be even more on their game once legally able to make more power moves.

"Nellie, what's the problem? Rah can handle himself and with Nigel there to have his back, you should be good. Just stay in the room with the baby and let them do their thing."

"I'm trying, Jayd, but Sandy's getting ghetto and trying to take Rahima out of the house. Rah's about to hit the roof."

"What's new? Rah's not going to let that happen and as usual, it'll take all night before Sandy gives up. Like I said, stay out of it, Nellie and the nightmare will end. I've got to go."

"But Jayd, these are drug dealers," Nellie says, speaking low as if she doesn't want to offend anyone. "What if they start shooting? I'm too cute to die young!"

Not long ago Nellie was all flirty-flirty with Trish's brother, Lance, who also happens to drag race his Mazda whenever he gets the chance. Like Chance and Jeremy, Rah and Nigel love to fix up cars and Lance's hot rod was definitely one of their favorite pleasure projects. I guess the fantasy's over for Nellie now that we know he's been with Sandy's nasty ass and I can't say that I blame her. Rah getting Sandy pregnant sealed the nail in the coffin for me and Rah's relationship back in the day, but I still think Nellie's overreacting just a bit.

"Lord, have mercy," I say, putting my forehead in my hands and rubbing my temples. Now I know how Mama feels when I get carried away. Nellie has a very active imagination when it comes to life in the hood. You'd think the girl didn't live in Compton the way she acts sometimes. I know she's been sheltered from death and destruction for most of her life, but really, the shit's not that deep.

"Nellie, you've been over Rah's house a thousand times. Has anything like that ever happened?" I'm not even going to comment on the fact that Lance and his crew only deal with herb, which is very different from being an actual drug dealer who makes crack and slangs heroin. They're not even your average weed hustlers. Lance attends a private university and is as preppy as they come. Nigel and Rah are not as preppy, but still clean with their gear and just as driven to utilize their hustle for bigger and better things.

"No it hasn't," Nellie says, slightly calming herself down.

"But I've never been over here without you or Mickey and they're arguing like it's about to go down. Seriously, Jayd, I'm afraid for my life."

I roll my eyes at the pink phone next to the book I'm supposed to be fully engaged in. Why is Nellie bugging me with this when I have more urgent matters to attend to? She doesn't even know what fearing for your life is yet. Seeing Misty's wicked grin put the fear of God in me and I've been through much worse.

"Nellie, if you're really that uncomfortable why don't you walk up to Simply Wholesome with Nickey and chill until it's all over?" I suggest. It's a good compromise and it'll hopefully get her off the phone. "Nickey loves to stroll and you still have about an hour before the sun sets. I'm sure one of our friends will come for you two when you're ready to leave."

"Walk? Are you joking?" Nellie asks, her fear of death obviously replaced by her aversion to physical exercise of any kind. I don't know how she ever thought she was going to make it as a cheerleader. "I'm not walking anywhere, especially not while pushing a stroller. As if."

"Bye, Nellie," I say, tired of this conversation. It's pointless trying to reason with my irrational friend.

"Jayd, wait. Maybe I should call the police."

Has Nellie completely lost her mind?

"No, don't do that. There's no need in everyone going to jail because that's just what'll happen if the law gets involved. Like I said before, hold tight and it'll all blow over soon. For real, Nellie, I've got to go."

"Fine, Jayd. But when you see breaking news about a shooting off La Brea Avenue, you'll regret not coming over when I asked. Good night."

Nellie hangs up in a huff as if it's my fault Rah has too

much drama in his life. That girl has ruined my concentration and my nerves right along with it. How can I focus when she's got me all riled up?

Before I can calm myself down my phone rings. It had better not be Nellie again. I don't want to have to go completely off on my paranoid girl to get my point across. Instead, it's my estranged boyfriend. I guess I'll have to face Jeremy one day. I can give him a second to apologize for the millionth time and then back to work. Maybe I can ease up on the attitude for both our sakes. I'm tired of being mad at my man, but I can't help my hurt feelings.

"Am I forgiven yet?" Jeremy asks. His voice is deep and tired. If he's as upset as I am about our separation I know he's losing some sleep behind it. If it weren't for my constant head cleansings, baths, and other spiritual work I wouldn't get any sleep either.

"I'm working on it." And I am in my own way. I'm not the best at forgiveness, but with the friends I've got I'm learning. "What's up?"

"Just in case you forgot, it's my birthday tomorrow," Jeremy says, jarring my memory. Celebrating his birthday was one of several things we had planned for his homecoming. "My brothers are having a little party in my honor tomorrow on the Manhattan pier. It would mean a lot to me if you could come."

"Jeremy, I'm not in the mood for a bonfire by the beach or anywhere else for that matter," I say, rubbing my temples at the thought of hanging with his surfer crew. I'm stressed enough as it is without adding another friend's birthday to the mix. And if Jeremy's older brothers are throwing the shindig then I know there's going to be twice the amount of alcohol and other stimulants present; I'm not in the mood to be anyone's designated driver.

"It's my birthday, Jayd. What kind of day would it be without my girl on my arm?" Jeremy pleads.

He can be pretty persuasive when he wants to, but I just don't know if I'm ready to go back to the way things were—and that's if Mama even lets me out of the house after I tell her what I saw in Misty's mouth. It's been an extra long day dealing with my friends and their bull, not to mention my temporary job for the rest of the week. The last thing I'll want to do after work tomorrow is deal with rich surfer kids who have nothing better to do but spend their time and money getting high. And I don't doubt Cameron's ass will be there.

"Oh, I wasn't aware Cameron would be there, too," I say, closing the spirit book. It's obvious I'm not going to get any more reading done. I'll just finish up my chores for the evening, take Dr. Whitmore's meds and call it a night. There's nothing like good sleep to help me put an end to this day.

"Jayd, come on," Jeremy says, exasperated. "Cameron admitted this was on her, not me. Why can't you just let it go."

"How am I supposed to let some shit like that go, Jeremy?" I ask, leaping to my feet. I could throw something I'm so mad, but I'll sweep the wooden floors instead.

"The same way I let it go when Rah kissed you at school," Jeremy says, reminding me of one of Rah's first pop-up visits at South Bay High last year. There have been other kisses snuck in since then, but Jeremy doesn't need to know about all that. "Not to mention that every time I look at your necklace or phone it gets a rise out of me. But I don't allow my jealousy to dictate how I feel about my girl because I trust you, Jayd."

Damn, when Jeremy puts it like that I guess I do have a lot to bow down to. Even if the kiss Rah planted on me was at the very beginning of me and Jeremy's courtship, Jeremy does tolerate a lot of heat from me. And he made me feel so special on my birthday that the least I can do is return the favor. Boyfriend or not, Jeremy's been a great friend to me.

"I haven't had a chance to buy you a present yet," I say, realizing I completely forgot to ask him what he wanted in the midst of my spiritual transformation and his kissing escapade. What do I get someone who has everything he could want and more?

"The only gift I need is you, baby. Promise you'll come." Damn, Jeremy sounds so sweet when he begs. How can I say no?

"Fine, but I can't stay for long. I'm not supposed to be out after dark until I'm out of whites." I know he doesn't get it, but knowing Jeremy he won't question my reasoning.

"Alrighty then." I can hear Jeremy's smile through the phone and it sounds good. "I guess that means you'd better get to the beach early tomorrow afternoon. The party doesn't start until sunset but we'll make a special exception for you, Lady J."

"See you tomorrow, Jeremy. And, happy birthday." I do feel a little guilty for forgetting his special day. Jeremy's the first of my friends to turn eighteen.

"Now it will be," Jeremy says, forcing a smile onto my face before ending the quick call.

I'm actually glad I answered Jeremy's call tonight. I miss talking to him. Maybe this is just what we need to find our way back to the middle. We fell in love at the beach and coming from Compton, I rarely ventured to the ocean before Jeremy came into my life. For all the drama we've gone through with his baby mama, Tania, and now this Cameron chick, he's brought more blessings than not, and that's what I need to focus on if we're going to stay together. Otherwise, the hood in me wants to take over and cuss him and Cameron out, which would be the worst thing that can happen. But best believe like Misty, I can show my fangs if Cameron steps to me at the beach or anywhere else. Like the saying goes, you can take the girl out of the hood, but you can't take the hood out of the girl.

~ 4 ~
My Two 'Hoods

Every 'hood's the same.

—ICE CUBE

The orange and red hues across the evening sky bring me a sense of peace and hope I'd forgotten about in the midst of my dramatic day. Pastor Godfry neglected to tell me that today was the mandatory parent-teacher conferences. I got paid to stay, so I did, but I wasn't all that happy about it. Along with each child's summer progress reports, we also discussed the benefits of the church's continuing extra-curricular educational support through our after-school program. I knew Daddy's church members were good at what they do, but I had no idea just how tight their hustle was and I must say, I'm impressed. Daddy's devoted female flock is a large part of the reason Mama left the church and never looked back. I can only imagine what kind of benefits Mama added when she played the role of First Lady. With Daddy's charisma and Mama's skills, I bet they were unstoppable back in the days when they were happily married. But like most relationships, Mama and Daddy have been anything but joyous for the past several years.

Speaking of drama, my homegirls have been working my last nerve all day long with blow-by-blow text messages about the madness that's been unfolding at Rah's house since yesterday. I'm sorry I couldn't be there for Rah and

Nigel last night, but Mama made it very clear for me not to engage in dangerous situations. Being around Rah's supplier and crazy baby mama I'm sure falls in that category. According to Mickey and Nellie, Sandy and Lance collected all of her belongings last night and after an unsuccessful bid to take Rahima with them, they finally left. Apparently Rah was so shook up about the possibility that he could not only lose his daughter again, but that Lance would also turn on him that he called his attorney first thing this morning to continue his quest for permanent sole custody of Rahima. I'm sorry it had to come down to this, but it's about time Rah finished what he started. Heffas like Sandy will never go away without some sort of intervention and a court order just might do the trick.

I'm actually excited to go to Jeremy's party, if for no other reason than to escape the never-ending soap opera that is my life. I need a break from the madness and being by the ocean always renews my spirit. I decided to hold off on telling Mama about Misty's new dentures until after Jeremy's birthday bash. Netta and Mama are at a ceremony tonight and gave me permission to attend the birthday party as long as I'm home on time. If someone else accompanied me from our spiritual family I could stay out later. But since I'm on my own as usual, I've got to be home before the clock strikes nine or the sun completely sets—whichever comes first. If I didn't feel like Cinderella before with all of the work I'm constantly doing, I certainly feel like her now with my imposed curfew before the party even gets fully started.

Finding parking on the beach this time of evening is a challenge. All of the Mercedes Benzes, BMWs, Audis, and other luxury vehicles are out in full effect enjoying the hot weather. The sun's shining brightly on the deep, blue sea, illuminating the surfers and sailboats in the distance. I know Jeremy and his crew are loving the high waves, which are rhythmically crashing against the shore reminding me of my initiation ceremony a few weeks ago. After being taken asunder by Yemoja I have a new and profound respect for the home of the elder orisha. I pray Jeremy and his boys have the same love for the power of nature because as with all things, the peaceful can quickly turn dangerous.

"Jayd, is that you?" Alia asks from her comfortable spot on a blanket next to Chance. They've got the best seat equidistant between the shore and the bonfire. She and Chance have been inseparable since his breakup with Nellie became official and I'm glad he's here. I want to see the look in his eyes when I ask him once and for all about the infamous picture. "You look gorgeous, girl."

I think she's the first of my friends to compliment my white attire. I opted for a long, linen dress with a shawl to cover my bare arms and sandals. I do feel pretty in this outfit. I'm grateful my mom did the majority of my iyawo shopping. She knows how to dress no matter the restrictions. If it were left up to Mama I'd sport nothing but wraps and T-shirts until my time was up.

"Thank you, girl. You don't look so bad yourself." I reach down and give my homegirl a quick hug before giving Chance a hug, too. They look quite settled in their new relationship and I'm happy for them. Nellie walked away from a good man leaving Chance free to get with his old girl and I'm not mad at him. Life's too short to sulk over some chick who didn't appreciate how good she had it, even if that chick happens to be one of my best friends. I hope Mickey learns from our girl's mistake before she's in the same boat.

"Jeremy and his brothers are in the water, but should be out soon to partake in the festivities," Chance says, already sounding quite lit. The rest of their school and surfer crew are sprawled out on several different blankets lining the shore chillaxing while watching the waves. "The sunset should be awesome tonight."

"Yeah, it should be," I say. I suddenly realize I've left Jeremy's gift in the car. I couldn't think of anything to buy him, so with my uncle Bryan's help I made him three mixed CD's of our favorite music and some new stuff, too. I know he'll appreciate them. "I left something in my car. If Jeremy comes over tell him I'll be right back."

Chance glances over his Gucci shades and winks at me affirmatively before settling his head back in Alia's lap. They both look as content as any new couple can be. If Nellie were here she'd shit a brick. She and the rest of my crew would be here but Rah, Mickey, and Nigel each have a lot going on this afternoon. Besides, they've never been much for hanging out at the beach, preferring to stay on dry land even if it is the last party before school starts this Tuesday. I'm just happy to be out of the house and free from working in the spirit room for a few hours. Feeling the warm sand in between my opened toes is exactly what I needed.

"Hi, Jayd," Cameron says, snatching away my good mood with her perky voice. This trick really has her nerve speaking to me after what I know she did. Nobody can say the heffa's a coward.

"What's up, loose lips?" I say, halting my trek toward my car parked in one of the various metered spaces on the street. The last thing I need is to have a confrontation with this bitch, but she came up to me, not the other way around.

Cameron's face turns as scarlet as the letter A she should be sporting on her barely-there chest. Before she can answer my inquiry, one of her friends who I recognize from school, but have never actually met steps behind her and whispers something in Cameron's ear, causing her to blush even more. They both giggle and glance back at the water where I see Jeremy and his equally fine brothers walk out of the water glistening like Greek gods.

I snap my fingers in Cameron's face demanding she stop drooling over my man and his relatives and focus on the ass whipping I wish I could give her. "Cameron, why don't we cut the act?" I ask, my body temperature rising with each beat of my heart. "I know you're vying for my man. And I know you made your move on him in Europe so don't even try and hide it."

"Jayd, I don't know what you're talking about, but I would never," Cameron begins, but I'm not listening to her lies this evening.

Her friend backs up at the angry black girl in her presence and I think that's wise because this sistah's about to blow— damn the party.

"Cameron, I have the proof on my cell that you kissed my man, so you can stop playing dumb. I also know for a fact that he didn't initiate or return the gesture." I pull out my phone and open it to the photo. As much as I've looked at the damn thing I should make it my screen saver.

Cameron turns pale at the evidence, but I don't buy her little act. Something tells me this chick is happy to see the picture in my possession. "How did you get that photo?"

"What difference does it make?" I ask, snapping the cell shut, now fully enraged. The sun's sinking into the horizon, which means I have to go soon. I'm wasting what little time I have left talking to this broad when I should be wishing my man a happy birthday. "I've got you, Cameron, and know this—you can't have my man, so back the hell up and stay out of our way before you really get checked, you hear?"

"Temper, temper, wicked girl," Cameron says, tilting her head to the right and smiling cunningly like she's got something on me. "We wouldn't want you to show your true colors out here where everyone can witness another one of your meltdowns." Pleased by my heated reaction, Cameron doesn't even bother pretending she's innocent any longer. What the hell?

"What are you talking about?" I ask, curious about how much she knows regarding my slight mental crisis this summer. If Nellie told this bitch anything about my personal issues I'm going to have her ass in a sling next time I see her.

"Let's just say I know better than anyone else here why you're wearing white, including your jaded boyfriend—no pun intended," Cameron says, her friend laughing at her weak wit. "Wouldn't it be interesting to see how Jeremy would react if he knew you went crazy while he was vacationing with his family?" How can Cameron possibly know what I did this summer?

I focus on Cameron's hazel eyes and jump into her mind before she can contest to the intrusion. I can't tell for sure, but somehow Jeremy's mother put her up to this. I knew Mrs. Weiner didn't like me, but this time she's gone too far.

"It's not going to work, Cameron," I say, watching as her thoughts unfold before me. "You can't break me and Jeremy up. We love each other too much to fall prey to your bull."

"Love is relative, Jayd. And it's not enough to change the fact that you'll never fit into our world."

Cameron's feelings for Jeremy are stronger than I realized. She's been infatuated with Jeremy since they were in grade school, mostly because her and Jeremy's moms fed Cameron the fairy tale of their youngest children one day being high school sweethearts and eventually married. Until I came along everything was going according to plan, including the shared family vacations. With our senior year fast approaching it's Cameron's last chance to make their fiction real as long as I'm out of the way.

Why do crows always make unnecessary problems? As much as Cameron's around the socialites of Palos Verdes, she should know by now their fantasies rarely turn out any better than the reality shows on television. Chance's mom had the whole Cinderella courtship and so did Jeremy's oldest brother, Michael, who married his high school sweetheart after stealing her from Reid's eldest brother. Both of those relationships are on the rocks with the wives and husbands proud alcoholics. That can't be the life Cameron wants no matter how fine my man is.

Before I have to slap some sense into Cameron, I'll opt for the nonviolent route and attempt to chill us both out instead. If I can cool her head maybe I can make the chick see reason. Feeling me at work, Cameron gets angry at my imposition forcing me to leave before becoming fully engulfed in her thoughts. I didn't get the whole story, but I got enough to know she's out for a rude awakening if she continues to side with Mrs. Weiner.

"You don't belong here, Jayd. Leave now before I humiliate you." Nearly hissing, Cameron rubs her goose bump–covered arms, looking toward the ocean where the party's finally getting started.

Jeremy waves at me with a concerned look, finally deciding to come for me instead of waiting for my return.

"Jayd, what's up?" Jeremy asks, walking up to me and kissing my neck. Sensing the tension between me and Cameron a few of his friends follow, including Chance and Alia. I guess most of them aren't used to seeing how we get down where I'm from. As far as I'm concerned I'm being real cool about the situation. Let someone try the same shit on Nigel and Mickey would have drowned the trick by now. Cameron should consider herself lucky I'm trying to walk a different path. Otherwise she'd be picking sand out of her teeth.

"Cameron was just telling me about how much fun she and your mom had on the trip while plotting the demise of our relationship, isn't that right?" I say to Cameron while holding Jeremy's wet waist. His black wetsuit is folded down halfway revealing his tanned chest and ripped six-pack. I dare Cameron to touch my man. Her fingers would be broken before she could beg for mercy.

"I was just telling Jayd she has it all wrong," Cameron says, her sly grin replaced by a look of pure innocence. "That's just crazy talk, Jayd. No one has it out for you and Jeremy, least of all his own mother and oldest friend," Cameron says without admitting to anything. Oh, she's good. I've gravely underestimated Cameron's manipulative skills. Best believe I won't make the same mistake again.

The setting sun brings a welcomed sea breeze to cool the heated environment, but it's not enough to calm me down. "And I was telling her to be careful about telling lies. The consequences can be very, very serious."

"Jayd, that's going a little overboard, don't you think?" Jeremy asks, obviously amused by the discussion, but there's nothing funny about Cameron's plan.

"Are you serious, Jeremy?" I ask, letting him go. "After all we've been through you're going to stand here and deny the possibility that I might be right?"

No matter which set of friends I'm dealing with, I get so tired of defending myself. The reunion was nice while it lasted, but as usual, Jeremy's quick to blame the irrational black girl in me for jumping to conclusions. That's our only real major issue and unfortunately it's a big one.

"She can't help being hood," Cameron's unidentified friend says, adding her unsolicited two cents. "She's a product of her environment." Whoever this broad is better take two steps back before she gets clocked by this so-called product.

"Come on, Jayd. I'll walk you to your car," Chance says,

trying to diffuse the situation, but I'm too hot to walk away with my supposed man defending the trick who's trying to break us up. I look at my homeboy and the fading sun behind him and decide to walk away for the time being, but I'm not letting this go.

"Happy birthday, Jeremy. I hope you and your new girl have one hell of a time."

"Baby, come on. Don't you think you're overreacting? You can't leave yet, please Jayd." Jeremy's pleading's not so cute anymore, not after what I just witnessed. Women can be very persuasive and as long as Jeremy second-guesses my skills I can't protect him from Cameron and his mom's ill intentions.

"It's getting late, Jeremy," I say, resuming my initial pace before Cameron intervened. "I'll send your birthday gift back with Chance. But mark my words, Cameron's up to something. I'd watch your back if I were you."

Cameron slits her angry eyes at me, waiting for my next move, but she'll never see it coming. If I have to deal with all of the other hackling hens in my world, one more makes no difference to me. All bitches have their disturbing ways, but their eliminations will be swift and exact, guaranteed.

Jeremy, his brothers, and their friends watch as Chance and I walk away, amazed at my claims, but I know I'm right. I know it's hard for Jeremy to accept that his mom's a treacherous wench, but truth is truth. I have to find a way to make him see the light. It's hard for Jeremy to deal with all the ins and outs of dating a black girl, but he's been rolling with it for almost a year. I know I'll never be from Jeremy's wealthy, white side of town and he'll never be a boy in my hood, but we've worked our relationship out for this long and I'm not about to let Cameron or anyone else mess us up. I'll do whatever I have to in order to keep my life from falling completely apart at the hands of the jealous wenches ever present in both our worlds.

* * *

A hooded figure in the night shadows startles me before quickly fading into the dark fog ahead. I'm standing in the middle of an intersection ready to make the sacrifice at the crossroads, but Legba's not here like he should be. Where's my daddy when I need him?

"I'm right here, little girl," a male voice says, but I can't see where it's coming from. The thick fog makes it impossible to see all around and the moonless night only aids in the ambiguity of my surroundings. "I'm always here, even when you don't see me."

"Trust your heart," Mama says in my mind. The hooded figure reappears as Mama's voice fades out. It runs down the street directly in front of me coming toward me and I stay put, bracing myself for the impact. I would run, but I don't know which way to go.

The fog slightly dissipates allowing me to make out more roads although I can't see any of them clearly. I run to my right and turn the corner only to see more roads and more hooded figures coming at me from several directions. None of my options are clear, but I have to choose one or get pounded by them all. Shit, now what?

"Legba, where are you? Baba, please help me," I cry, pleading with my father orisha to get me out of this mess.

The hooded figure turns to his left now wearing all red rather than the black ensemble he was just sporting a second ago. It's been Legba all along. Instead of feeling my dilemma, my baba laughs loudly at my confusion and continues moving my way.

"You never beg Legba, chile," Maman says, appearing on the opposite corner. I look up at the streetlight above my head and recognize it from the light at the end of our block in Compton unlike Maman's light, which is much older and unfamiliar to me. Most of the street signs are written in

French or Catholic saints' names. The intersection closest to
Maman reads St. Ann and North Rampart streets. I'm no ex-
pert, but I can recognize New Orleans locations when I see
them.

"How do I convince Legba to help me?" I ask, fearing the
impending collision seconds away. The red figures are gain-
ing speed, laughing more loudly the closer they get.

"You demand whatever it is that you need of him out-
right. That's the only way Legba will respect you," Maman
says hurriedly in my head. "Tell the truth and be loud about
it, omo Oshune. Then he'll give his child almost anything
you wish."

"Legba, clear the road!" I shout at the figures. I repeat my
demand, this time even louder and the sprinting red images
stop in their tracks.

"As you wish, my child," they say in unison with their
smiles evident under their hooded faces.

The fog finally lifts allowing the light of the rising sun to
clear all the roads before me. One by one, the Legba figures
melt away with the night darkness, making my decision an
easy one. My choices are clear; it's the execution that's diffi-
cult.

"Wake up, Jayd. It's time," Mama says, snatching me out of
my dream world and back to reality. What could be so important that my last Saturday to sleep in after working with
kids all week is over?

I rub the sleep out of my eyes noticing Mama and Netta
are up and already dressed. As Netta turns the dresser lamp
on Mama helps me to my feet. I don't know what time it is,
but the house is still quiet and I can tell it's dark outside.
Where did Netta come from and why are we up before dawn?

"Come over here, child. We don't have all morning," Mama

says, lighting the candles on each of the five shelf tiers instantly illuminating the small space.

Mama gestures for me to kneel before the small altars next to her bed and I follow her instructions, first wrapping myself in a white lapa matching those of my grandmother and godmother. I join them in the small space between the twin-sized bed and the family shrines with our backs to the wall. The window behind our heads is cracked allowing the cool twilight air to caress the back of my neck, fully waking me.

"So sa, so kere. Eshu Laroye, so kere," Netta chants to Oshune's personal Legba, saying that whether he speaks a little or a lot to open the shrine on a prosperous foot. Mama and I join in on the second verse, officially getting the spirit session started.

All living beings—the Creator itself and the other orishas included—has his or her own path of Legba. Whenever necessary all known roads of Legba should be recognized out of respect for the complex orisha. As in my dream a moment ago, Legba opens and closes all roads and is always the first and last orisha petitioned during all ceremonies.

Mama removes the outside cover of the spirit book revealing its aged, light brown leather skin. I've never seen the naked coat of the massive book nor the veve—or spiritual symbol—prominently displayed on the cover in red ink. The centered drawing looks like the letter x drawn through the center of a heart, much like the crossroads represented in Legba's veve.

"This is our lineage's veve, omo Oshune," Mama says, gently touching the paper with her fingertips. "The heart represents Oshune in her truest form, which is love and the cross belongs to baba Legba. As you can see in the drawing, there are several possibilities within those choices, sometimes good and sometimes not so good."

Netta looks at the book marveling at our mysterious family logo. "When and where the roads of our heart intersect is up to us. At best we are deeply flawed as humans, but Yeye still loves us anyway. It is through our mistakes our creativity thrives. Then and only then can our blessings begin and end with true compassion for others."

"The heart and cross are both drawn in red, symbolizing the power of love to give life," Mama continues. "And depending on the circumstance, that same love can take life away."

"And vice versa," Netta adds. "The lesson is to humble ourselves to the pain that comes with the blessing. Seeking wisdom in all situations is not an easy job, but ultimately it's the only one worthwhile."

I'm more confused now than I was in my dream a little while ago. With the week I've had dealing with Misty, Mickey's man, and Cameron's bull, the last thing I need is more to think about. I have enough work on my plate as it is.

"There are days where you will love your crown and others when you'll want to hurl it at your shrines." Mama looks at her altar grinning at her memories. "It's a marriage and much like in romantic love, you have to take the bitter with the sweet, Jayd. That's how all-worthwhile commitments are."

"You can try and cross a boyfriend out of your life, making him your ex and all that foolishness," Netta says, bringing the images of Jeremy with Cameron and Rah with Sandy to the forefront of my mind. "But once he cuts through your heart, those wounds are as permanent as a tattoo. It's always important to know which way you're going no matter the type of relationship you're engaged in. Ultimately to get to the sweetness, the sacrifice will be just as great as the benefit."

"We as children of both Legba and Oshune can have just

about anything our hearts desire, but it is in the asking where our deepest betrayal can also manifest," Mama says, taking the water glass from the ancestors' shrine and pouring a quick libation. "Yeye is about more than the material wealth that our gifts can bring."

Mama's always taught that same lesson repeatedly, warning of the dangers asking without giving could bring. That's why every time I buy something new I give something away. No need in being greedy when there's something better on the horizon.

"Deciding when to hold on and when to let go is the wisdom you'll master along the way," Netta says, claiming a brass bell from Oshune's tier and softly ringing it.

If I could share that lesson with my friends their lives would be much easier. Imagine how much time Nellie would save if she'd stop trying to be something she's not, or Sandy trying to hold on to Rah when he doesn't want her anymore. Those two alone could've shed five years of drama from their lives.

"There will always be decisions to make and consequences for every path you choose," Mama says cryptically.

"Do you want this man because he makes you happy or because having him will cause others to envy you?" Netta asks, the ringing growing louder with each thrust of her wrist. If she gets any louder she'll wake everyone else in the quiet house.

"Do you want this job because it is your true calling or because of the accolades it comes with? Are you a priestess because it is your birthright or because of the people who will worship your crown?" Mama adds, replacing the clear glass on the shrine while alluding to her evil counterpart, Esmeralda. I've yet to tell them about Misty's fangs, but will as soon as we're all done.

"Making tough choices is all a part of the ultimate sacrifice, Jayd, but know this. Love is God and God is love. It's as simple as that."

"Your grandmother's right about that," Netta says, opening the customary bottle of gin on the ancestor shrine and pouring out a little liquor in their honor. "People make life difficult, not the Creator. Spirit just wants to give and receive. After all, reciprocity is what life's ultimately about."

"This is yours to keep now, little miss," Mama says, handing me the delicate leather binding of the ancient text. "This is the cover you were born into. It's up to you to create and protect the next generations' stories."

"So it was never really damaged," I say, touching the smooth inner skin of the spirit book completely unphased by the damage my uncle caused to the protective coat.

"No, chile. As many times as we've been attacked we've learned how to protect what really matters. The outside is just for show."

"It's the heart and spirit that must survive," Netta says, slowly trimming the loose threads from the binding in preparation for the book's new case. "Flesh's purpose is simply to house the real deal."

Try telling Nellie, Mickey, or any of the rich girls we go to school with that bit of wisdom. As far as any of them are concerned what's inside a person, book, or anything else is irrelevant. If it doesn't look good it's not worth having.

"That's why this veve is such an accurate representation of our lineage, Jayd. Maman Marie designed it when she was initially ridden by her mother, beginning her initiation into the priesthood."

I trace the fine lines of the red symbol carefully feeling the ashe of the spiritual drawing course through my veins.

"Isn't it amazing how something so simple can have so much power?" Netta says, admiring the veve. Even with my great-grandmother's fancy and nearly illegible handwriting, it is a rather unassuming sign.

The people at the beach earlier this week whose cars costs more than most people make in ten years from around here have no understanding of that concept. Simple isn't in their vocabulary, which is why a lot of people I know aim to become hood rich: buying expensive rims for cars that aren't worth their weight in sand or buying flyy rides while living in their mamas' garages. It's all show with no real substance; quite the opposite of what we've got going on in the Williams' household.

"When Maman would perform her healing dance in Congo Square in honor of our ancestors, including the Maries before her, this was the veve she drew on the ground in cornmeal to begin the ceremony. Then, she would pierce the tip of her left index finger with Ogun's blade and let three drops of her blood lend ashe to the festivities.

"Every priest has their own version of the various veves for the orisha. This is ours and like any brand, it's recognized all over the world as the symbol of the Williams Women," Mama says, placing my right hand on the spirit book like I'm being sworn into office. "When you sign your name to this book you take an oath to protect our bloodline. Do you understand your responsibilities as a fully initiated voodoo priestess?"

"Beni, Iyalosha," I agree in Yoruba. Part of my training has been learning more French and Yoruba, our mother tongues. Sometimes Mama only speaks and answers in one of the two languages.

Mama then opens her brass Oshune vessel at the top of the shrine and takes out an eleke with gold, amber, yellow, orange, and red beads similar to the one I'm wearing now. At the end of the long necklace hangs a small charm with the crossed heart veve made out of solid brass. With the thin gold circle at the top of the heart connecting it to the string of beads it almost looks like a miniature purse. She sets the necklace on top of the veve in the spirit book and prays over it.

Netta passes Mama one of Ogun's blades—the orisha over war and justice—from the tier dedicated to the warriors repeating the same chant.

"Your first step as a priestess is to willingly surrender to the collective ashe of all the Queen Jayds before you," Mama says, holding the blade over the holy jewelry. "Give me your left index finger."

I raise my hand causing the jade bracelets to clink one by one down my arm providing the perfect accompaniment to their melody. The unfamiliar words become louder, lifting my spirits as tiny drops of my blood drip onto the faded yellow page where all of the women who came before me have already signed.

With my fingerprint firmly planted next to my name, the praying ceases. Netta wipes the blade clean with a wet towel while Mama claims the consecrated eleke. "Wear it well, my dear."

"It's beautiful. Thank you," I say, kissing the necklace before bowing my head for Mama to put it around my neck.

"You may wear colors even though you are still iyawo Oshune for the rest of your year." Mama kisses my forehead and smiles down at me with pride in her green eyes.

"Your praise name for our mother is Osunlade. Oshune wears the crown, which you do, little Jayd." Netta kisses me three times with tears in her eyes before rising to her feet.

Before rising, Mama kisses my hands, cupping them in hers. "Protect your heart at all times, help those you love at all cost, and keep what's sacred to you close, like money in your purse," Mama says, winking at me as she repeats my thought nearly verbatim.

"And don't be afraid to defend yourself against those who

try to hurt you. Remember a blade cuts both ways; the pain they inflict upon you will be swiftly returned." Leave it to Netta to keep even the holiest of ceremonies hood.

"There's no life without love. Be discerning in who you choose to bestow with the honor of having a piece of your heart," Mama says, standing up and joining her best friend on the other side of her bed. "Be a soldier for life, honey, and life will be good to you."

Rising to my feet and coming around the bed, both elders bow and kiss their fingertips to my feet, honoring Oshune's presence on my head. I've been promoted from a child to a young woman overnight and it feels good. I know my new crown doesn't come without haters as Netta and Mama have so eloquently reiterated. I understand it's a natural progression. The more powerful I get the deeper the drama, and I'm ready for it all.

Social Promotion

Reality is catchin' up with me/
Takin' my inner child, I'm fighting for it, custody.

—Kanye West

A long with the majestic ocean view from nearly every angle of the sprawling campus, the smells of freshly cut grass and new paint welcomes us back to South Bay High. I'm in no rush to park my mom's car in one of several available spots in the half-empty lot, taking in the serene ocean air before the school day officially begins. There's still the matter of cheerleading to deal with, not to mention having Mrs. Bennett as my AP English teacher this year, Lord help me. Ultimately not even the disturbing thought of having that she-devil this semester could ruin my good mood this Tuesday morning. No matter how I look at the situation, I'm a senior and will be out of here in less than nine months come hell or high water. The first day of my last year in high school is finally here and I'm ready to get on with it.

I thought Saturday's unexpected graduation ceremony would be more eventful with at least an actual bembe to celebrate like the ones Mama and Netta help with on the regular. Unlike Esmeralda's ceremonies that mirror performances at mega churches that deduct members' tithes from their taxes, Mama keeps it simple in our spiritual house. Pimping ain't easy, but it sure is common across religious and cultural lines; Mama has no part of any of that nonsense. With or without the hoopla, the point is that I'm a priestess and I'm good with that.

Mama has freed me up to wear some color, but I still can't wear anything too dark, flashy, or torn. Luckily I got in a little shopping yesterday afternoon with Mama and Netta right by my side and secured a few new pieces for my wardrobe. This morning I opted for a pair of white jeans, a yellow top, and a pretty rhinestone belt to give it some flare. My sandals match my shirt and are the perfect first day back shoes. I'm not used to walking around the huge campus anymore and need to get back in shape for the school year.

Last year the first day started with a fight, not to mention the drive-by I witnessed in my mom's hood right before school started. Hopefully today's drama will be at a minimum, but knowing my life I seriously doubt it. I haven't run into Misty yet, but I did find out something interesting about her vampire tendencies. In order for her to keep up appearances Esmeralda has to continuously feed her the potion without missing a dose. If I can find the tainted medicine and replace it with a tincture of my own, I can keep Misty's teeth, eyes, and every other manufactured power she has in check long enough to figure out exactly what Esmeralda's working with. Dealing with Mickey's man and Jeremy's obsessed admirer will require a different approach.

Due to Misty's mystical transformation and because of what went down at the beach with Cameron last week, Mama and Netta decided it was best for me to sit out this year's birthday festivities and recoup for my first day of school instead. My social quarantine didn't stop them from having enough fun for the three of us. Netta and Mama have had more energy than they know what to do with since their summer road trip. And with Netta's sisters insisting on sticking around to help with the beauty shop for a few more weeks, Mama and Netta have had more time to spend on spirit work and pampering—two of their favorite activities.

"Sexy chocolate," Chance says out of his car window, scaring me half to death. The other forty or so students look at us and keep talking amongst themselves. Everyone's used to Chance's swag. He honks his horn and I wave as I continue walking toward the front gate of the parking lot. I need to stop by the main office and pick up my registration packet. Usually it would've come in the mail at my mom's friend's house in Redondo Beach, but she swears she called and there was nothing there from South Bay High.

The rest of my friends should be here soon. I still can't believe we made it to senior year. No one I know wants to be late for the first day with the exception of maybe Jeremy. He called me consistently all weekend, but resorted to sending random messages by yesterday afternoon. We've been texting back and forth defending our separate stances on Cameron and his mother plotting Jeremy's future. Eventually he'll see I'm telling the truth. It's just a matter of time before I reveal Cameron for the diabolical trick she is.

"Hey, girl. I almost didn't recognize you," Nigel says, rising from the bench he and my girls are posted on and hugging me. The senior quad is full of freshly dressed students; a few of them who we all know shouldn't be here. Because South Bay doesn't want to look bad holding back dozens of students, the administration promotes some of them to the next grade even if they're not academically progressive. Makes me wonder why I work my tail off to get good grades when I know there's little chance I won't make it to the next grade level.

"There's the Jayd we all know and love." If Mickey only knew how much I've changed this summer she'd eat her words. "Flyy hair, colors and all."

Nellie and Mickey continue complimenting our individual outfits while also judging everyone else's. I feel slightly strange wearing colors again. It still feels as if all eyes are on me even though I know they're not.

"How come you know that?" my mom says, up in my head early this morning. *"No matter how you look, you'll always have je ne sais quoi . . . that something special about yourself that speaks louder than any outfit you're wearing. You could have on a potato sack and my daughter would still make heads turn."*

"Good morning to you, too, Mom," I think back while trying to pay attention to the fashion police in front of me. My girls are ruthless when it comes to gear. In their very separate ways Nellie and Mickey could run very successful clothing lines—Nellie for the preppy and loaded, Mickey for the hood-funky and fabulous.

"Good morning, baby. I just wanted to wish you a happy first day, miss senior in high school."

I know my mom's proud of her baby. Mama also called me before my alarm went off to say our morning prayers and wish me a good day. It was our first night apart in weeks. I missed sleeping in Mama's room like I've done most of my life, but I missed the privacy at my mom's place even more.

"Thanks, Mom." I would remind her that I have to make a special trip to the office before class due to her missing follow-up skills, but I stop short of getting cussed out before she leaves my head.

"Earth to Jayd," Nellie says, snapping her manicured fingers in front of my face. "What do you think of Misty's new haircut?" Nellie calls my attention to Esmeralda's favorite drone entering the quad. Misty's dyed her long, golden-brown, curly hair black, had it straightened and cut it to her jawline. With her crystal-blue contact lenses making the change even starker, her tight black dress and silver heels give Misty a completely different look altogether.

"Damn," Nigel says, expressing our sentiments exactly. Misty looks like a grown-ass woman. She already had that whole Boricua morena energy going for her, but instead of looking like Jennifer Lopez's younger sister, Misty looks like she could be one of her industry rivals.

"Close your mouth, fool," Mickey says, smacking Nigel in the back of the head. The warning bell rings saving us from envying Misty's transformation. We have to give props where due and to my crew and everyone else gawking, Misty's worthy. In my mind, we should all praise Esmeralda for a job well done.

"I have to go. I'll catch up with y'all later," I say, responding to the rush of energy from more students arriving filling the other quads, walkways, and buildings. There are some new faces; mostly freshmen and they look like it, too. There's no mistaking the young, fearful face of a new high school student. There's a reason we call them "freshmeat"—they're easy targets for all kinds of cliques, clubs, and everything in between.

The Associated Student Body is already passing out thousands of flyers trying to recruit new blood for their political regime. As president of the African Student Union, I need to call a meeting as soon as possible. We need to get the word out about our club, but first things first. I need to get my class schedule and get to first period on time. Being late is not a good start for the year.

As soon as I step foot in the front office the first day jitters hit and I'm suddenly nervous about everything from my new class schedule to where my locker's going to be. It's bad enough I automatically have to take Mrs. Bennett's English class because I'm on the Advanced Placement track, but I also have to suffer through cheer practice with the perky broads on the squad. It's been nice having a forced break from them, but all that'll change now that school's back in session.

"Jayd, it's nice to see you," Mr. Adelizi says, standing in front of his opened door with a stack of envelopes in his left arm. I rarely see him outside of his cramped office. "How was your summer?"

"It was cool," I say, returning the polite conversation while he flips through his load. "Busy, but good."

"How's cheer working out for you? I can't wait to see your completed college applications." Him and me both. And as for cheer, I'll avoid having that conversation with Mr. Adelizi for as long as possible. He submitted my name at the end of June for the program funded by the local colleges and universities to recruit the top students from local high schools. I did my part in order to get on the list by adding more activities onto my already full school plate, almost losing my mind in the process.

"It's going." I don't even want to think about all the work I have to put into applying within the next few weeks. Part of the program is paying for the applications so at least I don't have to worry about that. The application's just the beginning. The essay and exams are my biggest concern.

"Good to hear," Mr. Adelizi says, handing me the information I was coming for without my asking. Somebody had his Wheaties today. "I advise you get on your personal essay pronto. I'm sure you have a very interesting story to tell, coming from an underprivileged background and all." Why do white folks always think that kids from Compton are less privileged than they are? Money's not everything.

"Yeah, I'll do that. See you around, Mr. Adelizi." I've had enough of this uncomfortable conversation to last me a lifetime.

My background's interesting, but not just because of my

zip code. If I really put my life story on paper—voodoo priestess, crazy friends, and all—it would be a *New York Times* best seller, forget the college application.

"Have a good first day and don't hesitate to drop by my office if you need anything else." I open the manila envelope with my name and grade in the top right-hand corner. It looks good in print.

"Thanks, Mr. Adelizi," I say, speed-walking toward the main hall to check out my new locker assignment before heading to my first class with Mrs. Bennett. I can't believe I have to start every day off with her. I know this is some sort of test and like I said when I signed my name in the spirit book, I'm ready for the challenge.

The main hall is loud with chattering students, bouncing basketballs, and slamming lockers. Making it down the packed corridor isn't going to be easy. On the way to my locker I bump into my school mom, Ms. Toni, who's always a welcomed sight for sore eyes. Her office is housed inside of the ASB office in the center of the hall. I don't know how she deals with hundreds of students all day long, but I guess she wouldn't be the Activities Director if she didn't like the excitement.

"Jayd, baby. How's my girl doing?" she asks while wrapping me up in her warm embrace. It's so good to see her. I wish we had time for a good visit but I can't get off my mission. I'll be damned if I give Mrs. Bennett the pleasure of marking me tardy from jump.

"I'm good, Ms. Toni," I say, stepping out of the stampede before we get knocked down. "How are you?" The faint smell of cigarettes tells me I still need to see about making a potion that'll rid her of the nasty habit. I'll get on it this week when I check on solving Mickey's issues.

"I'm blessed. Come see me soon so we can catch up," she says, unlocking her office door. "There's something different about you, I can tell." Ms. Toni's very intuitive. That's one of the things I love about her.

"Yes, ma'am. Have a good day." Ms. Toni closes the door behind her and I rejoin the mad dash to first period. There's no time like the present to dive right into my destiny. Misty, Mrs. Bennett, Cameron, and any other haters in my path can't keep me from doing me. Knowing they're out there is half the battle; being prepared for their attacks is the other.

Against all odds I've been on time to first period the past few days. I'm glad the week is finally coming to an end. It's been quite hectic as usual, but having Mrs. Bennett has been more than a challenge—it's a prison sentence. I feel like I'm doing time for a crime I don't remember committing, and until I fulfill my debt to society I can't move on.

The spirit book said something about being challenged as an iyawo in more ways than we can imagine and so far that's the gospel. Taking care of my new personal vessels at my mom's house has been hard for me to balance with my stack of college applications, school, and spirit work. I'm used to taking care of the family shrines with Mama and the ones at Netta's shop. But having my own to be responsible for is more than a notion. The vessels are a manifestation and constant reminder of my path. Each container has its own special requirements and days for cleaning. I fully understand what Mama meant by stating the orisha are living beings. Consecrated vessels on a shrine are like having pets that have to be fed, cared for and they demand your time.

My mom's been pretty supportive of keeping my shrines in her apartment even if her fiancé is not fully aware of my mom's lineage. If Karl walks into her bedroom now and sees the small shelves dedicated to my ancestors, the warriors, and my head orisha, Oshune, and as well as to my father orisha, Legba, behind the front door he's bound to know something's up. I don't know why my mom doesn't come out and tell the brotha what's up. Karl's going to have to get used to the fact that we are voodoo priestesses from Compton by way of New Orleans if he's going to marry into this family. If my friends can deal with it so can my mom's.

Mickey's relaxed a bit after I helped her cast a protection spell on the scarlet letters from her ex-man. Until I can figure out something else to do, the best thing is to keep him from harming us. I wish I could make something similar to keep Mrs. Bennett from riding my ass. All of the new textbooks didn't come in on time so we've had to copy our assignments off the board. The rest of these high-tech junkies have laptops and other personal note-taking tools while my pen and pad have been doing the trick. Mrs. Bennett's notes, of course, grew in length as the week progressed, but I've got her today. After playing with my phone last night I discovered it records voice notes. It may have taken me until Friday to figure out a counter move, but that's okay. Slowly, but surely I'm learning the game.

"Before you get too comfortable there's a summons for you in the front office." Mrs. Bennett says, stepping into the room with a smile on her face. She hands me a yellow slip and points toward the door.

"What's this all about?" I glance around the buzzing class and rise from my desk. I can't be in any trouble. I made it all the way to Friday without doing anything to Misty or Cameron and should be rewarded for my good behavior.

"You'll see when you get there. And don't forget to take your things with you." I don't like the sound of this. Mrs. Bennett's too sure I'm not coming back.

On my way out I pass up Laura and Reid entering the classroom with Cameron right behind them. Cameron looks at me and then quickly diverts her vision down. I'll handle her guilt-ridden ass later. I've got to see what type of drama's waiting for me now.

"Jayd, where are you going?" Jeremy asks, stopping me in the main hall. I've skillfully avoided alone time with him all week. But as fate would have it, we're in the vast space all alone. The bell for first period rang a few minutes ago clearing the hall of any stragglers.

"I've been called to the office," I say, waving the slip in the air. "What about you?"

"I left my books in my locker." Jeremy walks up to me and touches my forearm sending chills up my spine. There's something about Jeremy I can't help but crave, but I also can't get the sight of him and Cameron kissing out of my mind. I wish he'd never gone away for the summer. Now everything's different and I don't know if we'll ever find our way back to the center.

"I've got to go," I say, continuing my trek to the principal's office. Jeremy looks sad, but lets me go.

"We've got to talk one day, Jayd. You can't avoid me forever," Jeremy says to my back as I enter the double doors leading to the main office where the administrative offices are held.

No, I guess I can't run from Jeremy forever, but I'm sure going to try to avoid talking to him without the proper ammunition to prove I'm right about Cameron. Until then, I have nothing more than the necessary polite words to say. I wish I could put my arm around Jeremy's tall frame and kiss his soft lips until this all blows over, but there's no downtime when bitches are plotting my ruin.

The main office is unusually full of students this morning. I guess there's a lot to get straight at the start of a new school year with schedule changes and other paperwork to deal with. I'll wait my turn like the other students in line at the principal's office. It makes me feel better knowing I wasn't the only one sent for this early in the day.

When I finally make it to the front of the line, one of the secretaries I don't recognize calls me to her desk. "Miss Jackson, what is your home address, please?" the secretary asks, looking down at the file in front of her. Why do I feel like I'm on the witness stand? Maybe it's because I'm perjuring myself and we all know it.

I repeat the Redondo Beach address my mom uses to keep me in the district, subconsciously giving her the wrong zip code.

"I meant 90278," I say, correcting myself, but it's too late. That little slipup is just what she was apparently looking for. She takes a fat, red marker from the pen jar on her neat desk and puts a huge checkmark on the front of the folder adding it to a small pile to her left. What the hell just happened?

"Jayd, your guardian needs to be here first thing next week," she says, stamping a letter with my mom's name on it and handing it to me. "She will need to bring current proof of residency as well as sign a sworn affidavit stating that you do indeed live within South Bay High School's zone. Enjoy your day." Damn, my mom's not going to be happy about this shit.

"You're damn right I'm not happy," my mom says, screaming in my head. I guess she heard everything.

"But it was a setup," I mentally whine, but my mom's not feeling my pain.

"Of course it was. And because you were distracted thinking about that silly boyfriend of yours you missed the trap laid out right in front of you. Shit. Now I have to take the morning off work to drive all the way to the beach. Do you know what that salty air's going to do to my hair?"

"Mom, my educational future is on the line and you're concerned about your press and curl?" I think back as I

make my way out of the office and back into the hall. In about two minutes this same empty space is going to be crawling with people.

"Whatever, Jayd. Bye," my mom says and I'm thankful she's out. The last thing I need after being bamboozled is being made to feel worse about it.

I'll get my books for Spanish and head to class early. It's always nice to see Mr. Adewale. I'm glad I have two classes with him again this year and my drama class hasn't changed, either. Cheer starts up again next week and this week we've been in the weight room working out. It's been a welcomed reprieve from the norm. The only class that's still up in the air is math and that should be settled by Monday. Apparently it's hard to find good Math teachers.

"What up, Virgin Mary?" Misty says, catching me off guard as she exits the girl's bathroom near the middle of the hall. My locker's on the other side and in order to get there I have to pass up this wench. My good week is officially a thing of the past.

"Do you mind? Some of us have better things to do than hang out between classes." I attempt to walk by, but Misty steps in front of me blocking my escape.

"Nice necklace," she says, attempting to touch my eleke with my family's veve.

I back up, which amuses the hell out of my nemesis.

"Nervous aren't we?" Misty asks, smiling wide to show off her fangs. Does KJ know he's dating a succubus? She's had him under her bootylicious spell since last year so he probably doesn't care as long as she keeps quiet and lets him do his thing.

"What, Misty? You think you're better than me now that you've got new mouth bling? I could care less about your latest stunt via your evil godmother. You see, that's the difference between us. You've always strived to be something you're not instead of going out for what's already yours. So what, you've got a new grill? I've got a gift that's mine and it trumps your circus illusions anytime."

"Illusion? I guarantee if I bit your ass right now you'd feel it." Misty moves toward me more quickly than I've ever seen her short ass walk. The only thing that slows her down is the four-inch high heel boots she's rocking with her mini, blue sundress. Even pseudo-vampires have to humble themselves to stilettos.

"Try it and see what happens."

Misty stares at me and I glare right back unmoved by her threat. She may have a different look, but I'm the same chick she's always known around the block. Misty better recognize before she ends up hurt. Sharp teeth, acrylic claws, and all are no match for me once I see red.

"The time will come for you to humble yourself to the real voodoo queen soon enough, trick," Misty says as the bell for second period rings crisp in the massive space.

The almost deafening sound bounces off the metal lockers and concrete walls. Once it's gone so is Misty. She thinks she's so damned special now that she's got a dark strut about her. I'm just the girl to shed some light on Misty's fantasy world. If she thinks Esmeralda's anyone's queen she's more far gone than I thought. I touch the brass charm on my chest feeling the support of my ancestors. If it's the real voodoo queen Misty wants to see, her wish is my command.

~ 6 ~
Ghetto Snob

It's not fair to deny me of the cross I bear that you gave to me/
You, you, you oughta know.

—ALANIS MORRISSETTE

My clients have suffered gravely in my absence. Sistahs and brothas alike have been sharing their horror stories with me all day long about visiting other stylists. I've heard everything from my mom's neighbor, Shawntrese, getting her hair burned out to her boyfriend getting his hair pulled out. I get it. They missed my mad skills. The deserted feeling was mutual: my bank account missed having money.

"Do you have any more of that shea butter repair cream for my hair?" Shawntrese asks, touching the damaged area in the back of her hair. I told her not to put any heat on her hair and keep rocking twists for a while. But the woman she chose as my substitute advised her differently and now my homegirl is paying the price.

My cell vibrates with a text message from Rah. I pick the phone up from the table cluttered with hair products and check the text.

"We're taking baby girl to Simply Wholesome for her third birthday. Hope her godmother can make it. Peace."

I hope by "we" Rah's not including his estranged baby mama, Sandy. That girl can make even the happiest occasion feel like a funeral.

"I'll text him back later," I say, twisting the last row in Shawntrese's hair.

"You know you're going," she says, claiming my cell from my slippery hands and quickly typing Rah back without my approval.

"Shawntrese," I say loudly, snatching the phone up but she's already pressed "send." Damn, she's got quick fingers. Am I the only person who hasn't mastered texting? "I wanted to chill alone tonight."

"You can do that after you have some fun. It's Saturday night, you've been working since seven this morning and you don't have any other plans."

"How do you know what I've got going on?" I say, setting the phone back down on my mom's glass dining room table and tugging her hair harder than necessary. She can be so nosy when she wants to be.

"Because you spent the last two hours telling me all about the ho trying to steal your man. I know you ain't seeing Jeremy tonight and other than Rah, who else do you kick it with?"

I haven't told anyone about Keenan, my new coffee buddy. All of my crew met him at Rah's school event in June where Nigel was heavily recruited by UCLA where Keenan plays football. Everyone could feel the energy between me and Keenan, but they have no idea we talk regularly. I know he's working at the coffeehouse tonight and wanted to drop by for a while. I have work to do, as always, and could use the escape. I haven't seen Keenan for weeks and really need one of his calming hugs.

"That's not the point. I'm tired and have a long day tomorrow with heads back to back like today. I don't feel like leaving the house."

"Not even for your godbaby?"

Shawntrese is right. I know I'm going to Simply Wholesome even if I do get tired of Rah not making plans. Why is everything last minute with that dude? Now I have to run to Target real quick to get her a gift. Her birthday's not until tomorrow and I planned on hooking Rahima up after my last client. Keenan will have to wait because I can't be a no-show to the party nor can I show up empty-handed.

"That's what I thought."

I admire Shawntrese's overzealous attitude about anything, but sometimes she's a bit much. Maybe I should let her loose on Cameron's ass. By the time Shawntrese has her say, Cameron would bow down to Shawntrese's mighty mouth. She reminds me of an older, more athletic version of Mickey. She's not into the bling, but gangsta men are her preference and fighting before chatting is her way. The only reason I haven't told Mickey or Nellie about all that's going on with me and Jeremy is because Mickey's on probation and would get expelled for any confrontations, and frankly I don't trust Nellie's wisdom when it comes to dealing with the rich girls she emulates. Nellie wants to be a permanent resident of their elite clique so badly she'd do anything they ask. That reminds me I need to ask her if she knew about Cameron's true feelings for Jeremy. With nowhere else to go Nellie should be at dinner tonight.

The smell of curry and fried fish fills the packed parking lot on the corner of La Brea Boulevard and Overhill Drive. I always feel self-conscious about parking my mom's old ride in here with the parade of fancy cars shining there so clean. My mom's Mazda Protégé's in good shape but it's over fourteen years old and needs some bodywork. Other than that, there's nothing wrong with her car.

My friends have already arrived and ordered for the whole group. My last client took longer than expected because the fool came in without taking out his braids I put in five weeks ago. His hair was nearly in dreadlocks it was so matted. It took me two hours to take his rows out and wash that shit thoroughly. Of course I charged him an extra forty, which he had no problem paying, but if he ever does something like that again he's on his own.

"Where's the birthday girl?" I ask, walking through the opened glass doors straight to our table. I know my former coworkers aren't here on a Saturday night and the new people behind the counter are unfamiliar to me.

"Auntie Jayd," Rahima says, running up to me. I pick her up in my arms, kissing her soft, ketchup-smudged face. She smells like baby powder and Egyptian Musk—her daddy's favorite oil. I've taken to wearing the sweet scent on occasion myself.

"I see you finally made it," Rah says, kissing me on the cheek.

"Work is work," I say, letting Rahima down so she can finish her turkey burger meal. I greet the rest of the crew and join them at the table where my veggie chili dog awaits. I'm so hungry I'd eat almost anything they put in front of me.

"Jayd, hold Nickey for me for a minute please," Mickey says, passing me the chubby four-month-old before I can dig in to my meal. "I need to find her cold medicine."

While Mickey frantically searches through the overstuffed diaper bag, I balance my youngest godchild in my right arm while manning my food with my left hand. I'm the queen of multitasking when it comes to eating. Mickey needs to clean that thing out. It's got all kinds of junk in it that has nothing to do with the baby.

Finally locating the local drugstore's generic medicine Mickey realizes it's empty. "Damn it. I knew I forgot to buy something at the store."

"Mickey, why don't we try and find something natural for Nickey's runny nose?" I pick up a napkin from the table and wipe Nickey's nose clean but there's more where that came from. "We are in a health food store."

"I'm not giving my baby none of that shit," Mickey says, quickly forgetting that the reason she's back to good health is because of the natural remedies I secured for her both from Mama and Dr. Whitmore. Speaking of which, I need to pay him a visit now that I've completed his most recent round of prescribed herbs. Maybe I can take Nickey again and get her checked out while I'm there.

"Mickey, natural's the best way to go. We want to treat the cause not just the symptom," I say, again wiping my god-daughter's nose clean with a wipe this time. "Isn't that right, little mama?"

Rahima looks at the baby in my arms and breaks down in tears. I had no idea she'd be this jealous. But I'm sure she knows it's her special day and since her mama's not here, I have to do my best to make her feel like the princess she most definitely is. Rah and Kamal try to console Rahima, but she's not having it. Her daddy and uncle may be cool, but tonight she needs a mother's love.

"Come here, baby girl," I say, reaching for Rahima who reluctantly comes. I put her on my lap next to Nickey and kiss her cheek, wiping away the tears with my right thumb. Poor baby. She's been through so much in her short life and with her mama pregnant by the local drug supplier it's only bound to get more eventful. I hope Rah can secure permanent sole custody of his daughter. Only then will some of the drama in Rahima's world come to an end. I wish I could say the same for my problems.

When I got home earlier one of the cheerleaders on the squad sent out a mass text about cheer squad resuming its normal practice schedule Monday and that I didn't need to show up since I missed the last half of camp. I don't need anything else to deal with, but I can't let it slide. Mama told the administration of my unforeseen dilemma and all was good until now.

"Everything all right, Jayd?" Rah asks. He's always watching me whereas my girls are too busy talking about plans for their upcoming birthday bash to notice the worried look across my brow. Even Nigel hones in on my energy.

"My week ended on a sour note, that's all."

Rah and Nigel look at me, waiting for the rest of the story, but I really don't want to talk about it while celebrating Rahima's day. Kamal takes Rahima to get something to drink leaving me with only one baby to balance while I get my grub on. Mickey could take her daughter back, but I'm in no rush to give her up. Mickey and Nellie decide to go to the other side and look around the store while we continue eating.

"Spit it out, Jayd. What's wrong?" Nigel asks, dipping several fries into ketchup and stuffing his mouth. I know how he feels. The menu has the best healthy food I've ever tasted. I haven't seen any of my regular former coworkers although I am surprised the manager bitch, Marty, isn't here. Maybe Shakir and Summer finally got wise and fired her trifling ass. If it weren't for her I'd probably still be working here. But it's all for the best. Besides, I'm making way more cheddar working at Netta's and for myself than I could ever make here, even if they do pay well.

"Yeah, Jayd. You know we're not going to let it go." Rah smiles and touches my hand, reassuring me that I can let it all hang out.

"Well, basically South Bay High would like to kick me out

for not being a Redondo Beach resident and I gave them the ammunition to do it. Not to mention the fact that I'm also being forced off of the cheer squad for missing the last few weeks of camp due to my initiation. Like I said, a sour note."

"Damn, Jayd. I feel for you, shorty," Nigel says, rubbing my shoulder. "I got you, girl. Whatever you need. If you want to stay on cheer I'll talk to the coach. And as far as the residency thing goes, I'll see if he has any pull with the administration office as well."

"That's really sweet, but it's my problem and I'll figure it out. If my mom comes up to the school and resigns her original affidavit I should be okay with the residency thing. As far as cheer, I'm not even sure I want to stay on the squad."

"Girl, what?" Nigel asks, nearly spitting out his food. "You're the livest chick on that whack-ass squad. If we don't have you it'll suck. That's one thing I do miss about Westingle more than anything. We had the livest pep squad in the entire region."

Rah and Nigel both reminisce about the flyy black girls who can get their groove on and liven up the crowd.

"Damn, this shit was expensive," Mickey says, placing the paper bag on the table. "The food's expensive, the medicine's expensive. The owners must be balling off this place."

"Mickey, lower your voice," I say, looking around the crowded restaurant at the other patrons looking at us, but my girl could care less about what these pretentious people in here think. We're only a few miles from South Central, but the way these snobbish Negroes act in here you'd think we were in Beverly Hills.

"We should've gone to Roscoe's House of Chicken and Waffles. We could have fed the whole crew for half the price." Nellie and Mickey rejoin the table with Nellie claiming a sleeping Nickey.

"Roscoe's," I say, looking at the food in front of me suddenly uninterested. I haven't been to our favorite hood spot in far too long.

"A number nine with a buckwheat waffle and a Lisa's Delight," Rah says, calling out his customary order. I usually get the same thing. We each have our menu favorites.

"A moment of silence for a number thirteen with grits and cheese eggs, please," Nigel says, bowing his head and we all follow suit. "Next session, Pico and La Brea."

"Hell no," Mickey chimes in. "Let's do the Roscoe's on Gower. There are always celebrities at that one." Leave it to Mickey to make good eating about being seen.

"Hell nah, girl. It's too crowded in that tiny ass spot," Nigel says. "If some shit jumps off in there we won't be able to get out fast enough."

It's so hood to think of exit strategies, but very necessary. I've been in enough fights that I know to walk into an establishment always looking for multiple ways out. It's a necessary hazard of our environment.

"Jayd. How are you, girl?" Shakir, the owner of Simply Wholesome asks, coming in through the front door and hugging me before greeting the rest of our crew.

"I'm good, Shakir. You remember my crew," I say, gesturing around the table.

"Yeah, but it looks like it's grown," Shakir says, noticing Nickey sleeping peacefully in her stroller.

"Yeah, that's our baby," Nigel says, like the proud daddy he is. He couldn't love Nickey any more if she were his flesh and blood. But according to the State of California he might as well be. Nickey received her official birth certificate in the mail the other day and Nigel's signature is on it just like Mickey's. There's no going back now unless they take it up with the courts.

"Bless you, baby," Mickey says, wiping Nickey's nose clean.

Even her sneeze didn't wake the sleeping baby. I wish I could sleep that hard.

"We've got something to help with congestion," Shakir says, gently touching Nickey's booties. He's raised three kids of his own and has a grandbaby on the way.

"Yeah, I just spent my life savings buying it for her." Mickey doesn't hold her tongue for anyone, amusing Shakir. My mom says he hasn't changed since high school. She helped get me the job here and if I ever needed to come back I'm sure Shakir would let me.

"Well, had your friend here stayed with us you could've benefited from the employee discount," Shakir says, trying to make me feel bad, but I know I did the right thing.

"Yeah, yeah," I say, smiling at my former boss. He's as cool as they come.

"I'm serious, Jayd. We miss you around here and could use the help. Two people just quit the weekend shift and you know they're our busiest days."

"I'm not looking for a job, Shakir, but thanks anyway. Mickey and Nigel could use the extra cheddar."

My friends look at me in shock that I put their business out there, but there's no shame in working for the man, especially if that man is Shakir. He's a decent, conscious brotha, flexible with the work schedule when possible and he pays well. What more could they ask for in an employer?

"Hey, man. I've been following your football career," Shakir says to Nigel who's still stuck on the job thing. I know it boggles his mind that he may actually have to get a job, but when he spit out his silver spoon the easy life went to the curb with it. "Looks like you'll have your pick of Pac ten schools to choose from once you graduate."

"I hope so, sir," Nigel says, obviously flattered. "But I'm seriously considering UCLA."

"Glad to hear. I'm a fellow Bruin myself. Come talk to me next week if you want the job."

"Thank you, sir. I just might do that."

I knew Nigel and Shakir would hit it off. If Nigel decides to apply for the job I know Shakir will be flexible with Nigel's football schedule and probably even attend a game or two. Shakir's a proud alumnus of UCLA. His office is full of blue and gold paraphernalia to prove it.

"It's time for the cake," Kamal says, pointing at baby girl who looks like she could pass out next to Nickey. It is getting late and I have a long workday ahead. Usually Sundays are pretty mellow, but I have a lot of time to make up for.

"Perfect timing. After this I have to get home and sleep," I say, ready to dig into the round Dora the Explorer cake from Ralph's.

"Damn girl, you just got here." Rah looks at me and shakes his head. "I know you have to get your hustle on, but remember to make time to chill, too."

"Yeah, and make time to do your boy's head," Nigel says, touching his thick crown. "I've been rocking the fro and it's cool and all, but my hair fits better under my helmet after you braid it up."

Mickey rolls her eyes at our boy's attention toward me, and Nellie's too absorbed in checking out the brothas with nice cars walking in and out of the establishment. My friends are a trip and then some, but I wouldn't trade them for anyone else.

"Bet. Session, tomorrow afternoon and I'll bring the snacks, and the comb." I smile at my friends knowing they mean well even if they can be the biggest brats.

"Roger that, shorty," Rah says, smiling. He takes out a lighter for the three pink candles ready to serenade his little girl.

Adding one more client to my full agenda is more work

than I bargained for, but I know I can handle it. And with a chill session to follow it won't feel much like work anyway. Getting through the day will be challenging enough, but well worth it once I stack my cash.

When I arrived at Rah's house Rah and Nigel were busy in the studio playing video games while my girls were busy reading the latest celebrity gossip on the Internet. After a couple of hours playing Mortal Kombat, Nigel finally settles down and lets me braid his hair while Rah heads to his old room to check on Rahima. I like fighting games just as much as the next person to help relieve stress, but not while I'm working. There's no way I can work my healing magic and compete with fatalities at the same time.

"Do your thang, girl." Nigel says, leaning back in his chair with both of his arms folded across his chest and his eyes closed. There's nothing like someone's fingers massaging your scalp to set your mood right if she knows what she's doing.

I run my fingers through Nigel's pillow-soft, thick hair, allowing my ashe to lead the way. Unless requested, I don't predetermine the size or how many braids go into my clients' styles. I just go with the flow of their energy, and Nigel's is telling me medium braids straight back. He already washed and blow dried it earlier leaving me to strictly braid.

Nigel shifts in his chair, submitting completely to the process. I guide the thin-toothed comb through Nigel's full crown gliding it all the way down to the nape of his neck parting the first cornrow. I pull the strong strands tight purposefully weaving in my pattern. My signature braid style is a long, smooth cornrow with a neat part. The new vanilla coconut hair balm Mama and Netta whipped up yesterday will bring out the natural shine in the dullest of strands, not that Nigel has that problem. His hair is healthy and the balm only makes his jet-black tresses sparkle more while leaving my fin- gers smelling and feeling delicious. I feel like a carpenter carving an intricate pattern from his mind's eye into the wood using his favorite tools. By the time I'm done braiding I usually want to say thank you to the client for allowing me to create my art. In reality it feels that good to complete my task.

"I got next," Rah says, interrupting the dual healing ses- sion without stirring a relaxed Nigel. I know I'm on my game if my boy didn't budge.

"Not a problem." I can engage Rah without breaking my concentration, but would rather work in peace.

Hair styling is a profession and it's also one of Oshune's favorite things. By working in her clients' heads she's also carving out their destinies right onto their scalps. So for me and other priestesses of Oshune, doing hair is a way of doing our spirit work as well as reaping the monetary benefits of our blessing.

"You look like you're enjoying yourself, Miss Jackson," Rah says, recognizing the intense look in my eyes. I smile at my boy marveling at my craftsmanship. He's both jealous that I'm working on another dude's hair—even if it is his best friend—and happy to see me back at work. Rah was one of my first clients in junior high and since being back in my life this past year has remained a steady paying patron.

The doorbell rings and Rah goes back in the living room to answer it. "Nigel, you've got company," Rah says from the other room. I tap Nigel on the shoulder and he jumps to his feet hearing Rah call him again.

"Mom," Nigel says, stepping into the foyer. I walk in curi- ous to witness the interaction between the ghetto snob and her estranged son. I can feel both the excitement of a five- year-old boy wanting to hug his mommy and the tension of a man wanting to hold back. I feel for my conflicted boy. Mrs.

Esop looks equally confused about how to approach her alienated son.

"I just wanted to drop off these pictures. I wasn't sure of the reliability of the mail system on this side of town." Like she lives that far away. It's barely a ten-minute drive between the two hoods, but there is a significant difference in the home values from Windsor Hills to Lafayette Square, even if they're both a stone's throw from Crenshaw Boulevard.

"Thanks," Nigel says, taking the photos from his mom who stands nervously by the entryway.

Carefully sliding the pictures out of the large, gold envelope, we both smile at the photos we took at our final debutante dress rehearsal. The actual night turned out to be a disaster—quite the opposite of the picture-perfect couple presented here. We do look damned good in our couture outfits. Too bad Mama and Netta had to rip the gown off of me during my spiritual meltdown at the beach, but it's all good as far as I'm concerned even if I know Mrs. Esop sees the incident quite differently.

"Well, I see you've gone back to your old ways of braiding hair," Mrs. Esop says, turning her nose up at Rah's simple home. I'm surprised her bougie ass even ventured to this side of town, even if Windsor Hills is a lovely predominantly black community. The homes and yards may be more modest than the ones in her Lafayette Square community, but a snob is a snob, and Mrs. Esop is the queen of them all.

"What's that supposed to mean?" I ask, insulted. Hearing the conversation, Mickey and Nellie emerge from the back room and see Mrs. Esop who promptly rolls her false eyelashes at their presence.

"It means that after all of the money, time, and energy I spent investing in your coming out into the young lady I know you're capable of being you've still decided to remain in the same place you were before—nowhere."

"Now hold on just a minute, Mom," Nigel begins, but I tap my friend lightly on the shoulder to indicate I've got this one. Our showdown has been coming for several weeks and I'm ready.

"No, Nigel. Your mother's right," I say. "I couldn't agree more that the time spent preparing for the superficial initiation into a society I never desired to be a part of in the first place was a complete waste of time and energy. Not to mention all the money I lost attending teas and rehearsals when I should have literally been minding my own business."

Mrs. Esop glares at me like she wants to slap the shit out of me and I wish she would. Mama would fly over in one quick swoop and kick her ass all up and down Slauson Avenue.

"I knew you had it in you to be an ungrateful, little hoodrat like your friends, Jayd, but I had no idea you would so quickly turn on the hand that feeds you." What am I, a puppy? She's really got it twisted if she thinks I give a damn about her fake-ass world.

"You don't feed me, Mrs. Esop. What my mother and grandmother don't provide I give myself or haven't you noticed I'm well fed?"

Mickey and Nellie snicker at my sass, angering Mrs. Esop even more.

"Yes, I can see that your little business—if you can call it that—seems to be doing well and I'm glad to hear that," she says, pulling out an envelope and handing it to me. "In that case, you should have no problem paying me back for the dress that's mysteriously missing."

I pull out the receipt and itemized expense report she's so eloquently prepared and read the list.

"Eleven hundred dollars!" I scream. This bitch is crazy if she thinks I'm paying her back all of this money.

"Yes, and that of course doesn't include my expertise,

which I'm going to write off as the charity you're obviously still in need of. Good day," Mrs. Esop says, leaving me in complete shock. What the hell?

"Mom, you're being ridiculous, you know that, right?" Nigel says after his mother. "You going after my friend isn't going to bring me back home."

Mickey looks over my shoulder at the paper and shakes her head. This is some cold shit, for real. I knew Mrs. Esop was pissed, but I had no idea she'd come at me like this. And it wasn't my fault Maman decided to ride me that night. How am I going to get out of this mess?

"We'll see about that, Nigel. You know I never lose," Mrs. Esop says, approaching her immaculate Jaguar in front of the house. Even if she lives in a million-dollar home, she still takes her ride to Crenshaw Carwash like all the other ballers in the hood. A rich ghetto bitch is the worst kind there is, I swear.

"Mrs. Esop, you know I don't have this kind of money," I say, moving from the porch toward the curb.

"You should've thought about that before you decided to embarrass me and ruin my reputation," she says, rolling her neck and waving her hood flag high. There's the Compton girl we all knew was hiding behind her large Gucci bag Nellie's quietly envying. We know that purse didn't come from the swap meet.

"It was never my intention to embarrass you, Mrs. Esop," I say, trying to turn this situation around. Mama says you can catch more bees with honey than vinegar and I'm going to lay the sweetness on extra thick. "I'm very grateful for the opportunity you gave me and wish I could go back and do it all over again."

"Intentions paved the road to hell, Jayd. Maybe if you went to church you'd understand that instead of running around with that crazy grandmother of yours, doing God-knows-what with my couture gown. How dare you take my kindness for weakness? But I'll bet you'll never make that mistake again."

I knew the heffa could be mean, but I had no idea how vindictive she could be.

"Did you just call my grandmother crazy?" I ask, now on the passenger side of her vehicle. She takes her hand off the driver's side door handle and crosses her arms across her chest. I know she didn't just go there. "You crossed the line calling Mama out of her name."

"Lynn Mae doesn't have a name, but I do. And you abused it when you decided to go AWOL at the ball. But you will rectify the situation by paying me back every dime I wasted on you. End of discussion."

Mrs. Esop opens the door in an attempt to escape, but I'll be damned if she has the last word. Defiling my family name is not how it's going down today or ever, I don't care what she thinks I did to her or how much money she says I owe.

"You and I both know the power of words, and you just cursed yourself by slandering my grandmother's name. Remember that," I say, backing up from her ride.

From the look in Mrs. Esop's eyes I can tell I've put the fear of God in her and rightfully so. She went too far in more ways than one this afternoon, but bringing Mama into the mix was completely uncalled for. I may have ruined her dress and I'll own that, but talking about the Williams women is her bad and she'll regret her words—I'll see to that.

"Jayd, I'm sorry for all of this," Nigel says. Mickey's the one who should be sorry. Had she not given me the task of making sure Nigel's mother was present at her ghetto-ass baby shower, I wouldn't be in this mess. It was bribery, plain and simple. I never wanted to be a debutante in the first place, but for Nickey and her mama, I agreed. I was Mrs. Esop's little ghetto pet project and she relished in turning me from what she considered a hoodrat to a lady. What about my name? How dare she use me for her own reasons and then get pissed because it didn't work out according to her plan. What about my burden, my expenses, my time?

Maybe I'll compile an expense list of my own and then we'll see who owes who at the end of the day. I'll be damned if I'm going out without a fight, and I'm surely not giving her a dime of my hard-earned money. I worked too hard at her stupid functions to end up broke after it's all said and done. As usual, Mama was right when she warned me about dealing with Mrs. Esop. At the end of the day, all she cares about is herself. At least that's one lesson I can take away from this experience, that and never piss off a woman who has more designer bags than Mariah Carey. Mrs. Esop takes her time and money very seriously and in her mind I've wasted them both. Lucky me.

~ 7 ~
Bag Lady

*I guess nobody ever told you all you must hold on to/
Is you, is you, is you.*

—ERYKAH BADU

After the weekend I've had, I'm actually glad to get back to school even if Mrs. Bennett's riding me harder than a cowboy rides a bull at a rodeo. Lucky me, I get to start my day with the heffa of all heffas. Maybe if I bring her uptight ass an apple every day she would get the fiber she needs to get rid of some of the shit she's holding in. I wish I knew what I did to her so I can say sorry and get on with my life, but not a chance. She'd probably take my apology as insult to injury and throw it back in my face like Mrs. Esop did yesterday evening. Women like them don't want apologies; they want revenge by any means necessary.

All of this newfound tension in my life is taking its toll on my peace of mind preventing me from dreaming—good or bad. I didn't sleep well last night and getting up this morning was even more difficult. And with Ellen and the rest of the cheer squad at the forefront of my mind this afternoon, I don't foresee relaxing anytime soon.

"Jayd, fancy meeting you here," Ellen, the head cheerleader says as I enter the girls' locker room. I haven't been to cheer practice since my initiation and I know Mama took care of that for me no matter what that stupid letter said.

"What's so fancy about it?" I ask, placing my backpack and

purse in the unassigned locker and removing my new Nikes. I brought some clean clothes to dress out in and don't need an audience watching to change into them.

"Well, you missed the last month of camp," Ellen says, leaning her short frame up against the lockers across the bench. "We just assumed you weren't interested in being a Lady Hawk anymore."

"Well, as usual you know nothing about me or my interests." I finish dressing out and slam the locker door shut before removing the key with attached safety pin and attach it to my dance shorts. I have nothing left to say to this heffa.

"Today's the first day of practice before the pep rally Friday. Do you really think you're ready to perform in front of the entire school?" Ellen has a good point but she'll never hear me say that. She could offer to help me catch up, but she'd rather try and break me down. Too bad for her I'm not weak.

"I'll be ready by Friday, Ellen. Don't you worry your little blond head about it."

Ellen slits her gray eyes at me. "You're the only one who thinks you belong here, Jayd. This isn't hip-hop dance at the gym. It's competitive cheerleading and you're not a winner."

How dare this peppy pipsqueak tell me where and what I am. And I can't even deal with the hip-hop comment without seeing red. Now it's really on.

"Jayd, I didn't think you'd be here," Ms. Carter says, stepping into the locker room from the gymnasium door promptly saving Ellen from an overdue ass whipping. "Didn't you get my letter?"

Ellen smiles at the confrontation she's been waiting to see since she transferred from her high school in Dallas. From the first day Ellen and I didn't get along because she pranced in here like the goddess of cheer and was instantly handed all the power over the squad.

"Yes, I did, but I don't understand it." I open my locker and take the paper out of my backpack. "It says here the leave was unapproved, but my grandmother went through all of the right steps to validate my absence. Besides, Ellen was gone for weeks for her family reunion and she's still on the squad."

"Ellen's absence was pre-approved and she can miss days at a time. The rest of the squad needs practice." Ms. Carter can't seriously think favoritism is going to fly when we're talking about school absences. I will take this up with the administration if I have to, even if I'm already hanging on by a thread with them, too.

"Wait a minute," I say, stopping them both on their way to practice. "So, let me get this straight. It's okay if Ellen goes home to her family farm in Texas for the last few weeks of summer, but I don't get the same privilege, even when mine was an emergency not a luxury?"

"Jayd, the rules specifically state that the time off has to be pre-approved," Ms. Carter repeats. "And personally, I think your blatantly disrespectful attitude toward our rules in the past are indicative of your future behavior. We don't need you on the team any longer."

"Screw the rules," I say, unable to control my anger any longer. "I worked my ass off on this squad and everything was fine until Little Miss Lonestar came and screwed everything up."

"Jayd, language, please." Ms. Carter and Ellen look shocked by my outburst, but they shouldn't. This is crap and we all know it. That's why they sent me a letter over the weekend instead of telling me in person during the school week. They'd hoped I would let it go, but letting me sit on it all weekend was the worst decision they could've made.

"Whatever," I say, dismissing her request. "Ellen can cuss all day long and you barely blink at her, but when I speak the truth all of a sudden rules come up. You may think you've got a good case, but I'm not done—not by a long shot."

"You are for today. You can spend the rest of P.E. in the workout room. You're no longer on the squad, Jayd. Accept it and move on." Ms. Carter and her sidekick leave the locker room and join the rest of the girls on the gym floor.

Wait until Ms. Toni gets wind of this. I haven't made a big deal about the unfair treatment I've received since Ellen arrived, but I'm going to put my debate skills to use and win this battle. It's not even that I want to remain on the squad because in all honesty I don't care anymore. But right is right and they are definitely in the wrong for this one. I didn't even want to try out in the first place, but now that I'm here no one's pushing me out on a technicality. Hell no, not me. I'm going to take care of this myself and by the time I'm done, they'll know not to mess with Jayd Jackson again.

This afternoon's my first official day back at Netta's Never Nappy Beauty Salon. I've missed working with Mama and Netta. I've even missed the customers and the accompanying tips. But with Netta's sisters, Celia and Rita, still visiting from New Orleans, there isn't as much work for me to do as usual. Their presence has even forced Netta to spend more time making hair products and doing administrative duties with Mama. I think we're all ready for their visit to end. We don't get to share our days like we used to. And I need their wisdom more than ever this week. It's only Monday and I'm already in over my head.

"Mama, what's with all the paperwork?" I ask, eyeing the four bags full of receipts and bank statements she and Netta are carrying to Netta's truck parked in the back of the lot. I'm sweeping the back porch since all of my other tasks have already been done.

"It's time to do our taxes, little Jayd," Netta says, smiling as she pecks me on the cheek. I return the affection and walk around to the front of the shop to continue my sweeping where I see more bags.

"Taxes?" I ask. I thought they just worked on the sly like everyone else in our hood. The IRS may only have three letters, but it's a bad word around here.

"Yes, child. Taxes," Mama says, taking the last two bags and passing me by. "This is a real business, Jayd, and we've always run it as such. Speaking of which, how's your bank account looking these days?" Mama asks, forever in my business. To tell the truth, I haven't balanced my checkbook in months. As long as money comes out of the ATM when I need it, I'm cool.

"It's good," I say, wishing I could leave it at that but there's no chance Mama's letting my nonchalant answer slide.

"Have you thought about filing your own taxes next year?" Netta asks, coming around to the front and entering the conversation.

"I didn't know I could," I say.

Mama and Netta roll their eyes at me before claiming the last two bags and heading toward the front door. With two successful women as my mentors you'd think I'd have better financial planning, but I'm my mom's girl when it comes to money. She spends until she can't spend anymore. Then she checks her account balances, using whichever card she can to pay off another. And bills are on a need-to-pay basis.

"Rita, Celia," Mama says, entering the buzzing shop ahead of Netta and me.

"Lynn Mae," the two women say in unison without looking directly at Mama, who sucks her teeth as she heads to the shrine room/office housed in the back of the quaint shop.

I know Mama will be glad when Netta's sisters leave. They were supposed to head back to New Orleans a couple of weeks ago, but in light of my recent episode, they decided to stay and help Netta out at the shop a little while longer. Netta has been enjoying having her sisters around, but the longer they're here the further apart Netta and Mama grow. I guess drama between women happens at any age and even to the best of friends.

"Did we finish with the clients' orders?" Mama asks Netta who's now in the office filing the paperwork. There's so much that goes into running a business when it's done properly.

"Yes, Lynn Mae. Rita and Celia even stayed late to help," Netta says, ignoring Mama's disapproving glare.

"Good. There's always plenty of work to go around," Mama says, sourly. That may be true, but the last people Mama wants helping are Netta's sisters. Mama places her bags down near the shrine and heads to the bathroom to wash up before beginning her chores. I hug Netta and follow suit after Mama.

"Nettie, we're out of shampoo," Celia, the eldest sister says, entering the office much to Mama's visual disapproval. When the shrines are open only people who respect the ancestors and orisha should be present. Rita and Celia have no love for our way of doing things.

Mama kneels on the bamboo mat in front of the shrine to greet it before beginning her work. After washing my hands and face I join my grandmother and ignore the loud intrusion. Ever since the sisters arrived it's been less than serene around here, mostly because of the tension between them and Mama.

"Girl, what are you talking about?" Netta says, turning around in her swivel chair at her antique wooden desk and peering over her reading glasses. "There's plenty of honey-mango shampoo in the cabinets above the sink as well as the special tea tree and mint dandruff control for the clients who need it."

"I know that, Nettie." Celia looks at us before continuing. I can tell she wants to get closer to Netta but she'd have to cross in front of us to do it and that ain't happening. "I meant the shampoo we made. I think it's better suited for our style, don't you?" Celia asks, attempting to whisper her request but we all heard what she did and didn't say loud and clear.

"Celia, Lynn Mae and I have been using our products in this shop forever and all of the styles are compatible with our line." Netta looks at her sister oblivious to the insult still in the air. Celia doesn't want to use anything Mama's had a hand in creating.

"Yes, but Rita and I like the other brand better."

Netta looks at Mama rise from the mat and look squarely at Celia who looks like she wishes she could orb out of the room like on one of my favorite shows, *Star Trek: The Next Generation*. She had to know how much nerve she had coming in here and asking a silly question like that in front of Mama. Some people just ask to be checked.

"Celia, if you don't like our products feel free to make more of your own," Mama says, before turning around and closing the sheer curtains covering the tall shrine. "But get it straight, this is our shop and we do things our way here."

Mama walks past Celia, who's really feeling herself today. I guess she's been here so long she's forgotten Mama's as much a partner in the shop as Netta.

"Yes, but just because something's been done one way for a long time doesn't make it right. Now, like I said, we need more of the other shampoo. Rita and I will get on making another batch as soon as we finish the three clients in the front. Jayd, why don't you get the broom and start sweeping up the hair, dear. It's been a busy morning."

Mama stops in the hallway and turns back around. Netta looks at me urging me to stay put knowing Mama's about to blow and there's nothing either of us can do about it.

"Jayd's not your servant girl, Celia," Mama says, placing her hands on her hips and propping her head to the right. "She's a talented apprentice who does a lot more around the shop than sweep."

"She's a child and she shouldn't be allowed anywhere near the clients until she has her cosmetology license," Celia says, boldly speaking out the side of her neck.

"Who the hell do you think you are to come into my shop and dictate how I teach my granddaughter the family trade?" Mama asks at the top of her lungs. "Netta, you'd better get your kin."

"It's not your shop, it's Netta's and we as her blood have a say in what goes on around here, especially if it's unethical."

Netta steps away from her desk and joins her sister across the room in an attempt to silence her. If we continue down this path it can only end in tragedy. Celia should've never brought me into the mix no matter how she feels about a minor washing hair. Technically, as long as I don't handle the actual styling I'm considered an assistant. Once I hit sixteen I was old enough for that job title, but I don't need to set my elder straight—that's Mama's job.

"What's all this fussing about? We've got paying customers out front," Rita says, charging into the back room. It's too late for damage control.

Mama walks toward the door and closes it to keep the clients from hearing any more of this discussion, probably because it's about to take a turn for the worse.

"I'm only going to say this once, Rita and Celia. After that it will be up to your sister to make the final call."

Mama picks up the clay plate holding one of the seven Legba shrines in the shop and continues.

"I have been a partner in this shop since Netta and I came to Compton over thirty years ago. We've been blessed to be able to handle the business on our own, and with Jayd working here this past year we've been more productive than ever before."

"Yes, Jayd has been a welcomed addition to our staff. I can't remember what the shop was like before she came along," Netta says, backing Mama up. I hope she's not forced to choose between her sisters and Mama, but that looks like what it's coming down to.

"Three women. That's all this small space can handle," Mama says, putting up three fingers on her free hand, holding tight onto Legba with the other. "It's either the three of you or the three of us."

"Lynn Mae, what are you saying?" Netta says, leaving her sister's side and walking up to Mama.

"I'm saying that there's not enough work to do for all of us. Someone's got to go. Jayd, get your things. We have work to do at home," Mama says, replacing Legba's clay vessel in the corner.

I open the door and head to my cabinet in the front of the shop where my purse is. The three customers under the still dryers pretend not to be interested in us, but can't help staring as Mama and I charge out of the shop.

"Lynn Mae, wait a minute. Don't leave upset. It's not good luck," Netta says out the front door, but it's no use. Once Mama makes up her mind it's a wrap.

Mama's across the street and halfway up the block by the time I get the car started. I wave bye to my godmother and hope this won't be my last day working at the shop. I'm confident Netta will choose Mama in the end, but blood is thicker than water, no matter how strong the friendship. I hope in this case the old saying is wrong.

It didn't take long for Netta to call Mama with her decision. Netta politely asked her sisters to go home. According to Mama they took it personally and left in a huff. I'm just glad they're gone so things can get back to normal around the shop. After Netta's sisters finally made their exodus Monday night, Mama and Netta wanted the shop to themselves on their regular Tuesdays to cleanse the air. I needed the afternoon off yesterday to catch up on my schoolwork. There's more reading in my English class than necessary and Spanish hasn't been easy, either. No matter if it's my favorite teacher or my most hated, work is work and South Bay High gives plenty of it.

Math is my third class and probably the worst of them all. I know nothing about statistics nor do I want to. But it's a senior math class and because I didn't do well in Algebra or Geometry my sophomore and junior years, I have to take another upper level Math class this semester in order to graduate. My saving grace is the fact that I again have Mr. Adewale for Advanced Spanish second period and for Speech fourth. Fifth period is Drama class, as always and depending on how things go with Cheer, P.E. will remain my last class of the day.

With all of the books I'm carrying this semester it's a wonder my back hasn't snapped under all of the pressure. My locker's already packed with useless flyers and other information signaling the need to clean it before the day is over. After my speech class this period I can take a minute to handle some housekeeping at lunch. Nellie and Mickey have been busy planning their party Saturday and I'm tired of hearing about it. And my boys have been in their own worlds, battling each other on the Nintendo DSI's. Without Jeremy, life has been pretty boring around campus this week.

"Little Miss Jayd," Ms. Toni says, patting my back causing me to jump a bit. I didn't hear her come up behind me in the busy main hall. It's the passing period before fourth and everyone's moving quickly to get to their next class.

"Hi, Ms. Toni." I finish changing out my morning books and close my locker shut before hugging my school mama. "How are you?"

"I'm doing just fine, Jayd. The real question is how are you?" By her tilted chin and piercing eyes I know she knows I've had a difficult week.

"So, you heard about cheer, huh?" I ask, walking her to the Associated Student Body office in the middle of the vast hall. I don't see how she deals with students running in and out of her space all day, but she does close her office door when she needs a moment to herself.

"Yes. And what I want to know is why didn't you come to me when you first knew you were in trouble?"

"This all went down Monday afternoon. I planned on coming to you at lunch to see if you were available to talk."

"For you, always," she says, opening the door to the massive room and letting me in. "Since you're here now let's chat for a few minutes while it's quiet. I'll write you a pass for Mr. Adewale's class."

During fourth period most of the ASB students are passing out flyers and doing announcements for various events, like the first pep rally this Friday that I should be performing in, but probably won't be allowed to. Too bad, I really like the dance routine and I'm good at it, too—minus the gymnastics.

"Thanks," I say, taking a seat across from her well-organized but packed desk.

"Well, are you going to tell me what really kept you away from cheer camp for the last few weeks or do I have to guess?" Ms. Toni asks, propping herself on the corner of her desk.

I take a deep breath and decide to tell her the truth. "I was formally initiated as a voodoo priestess. It wasn't planned and couldn't be avoided."

Ms. Toni looks fascinated by my confession. I can tell she has all kinds of questions, but doesn't want to pry and I'm glad because that's about all I can tell her.

"I see." She takes out a manila folder with my name on it from her desk and passes it to me. "Ms. Carter has formally called for your withdrawal from the cheer squad effective immediately."

I open the folder and read the form myself ever amazed at how swiftly knives can appear in my back. Shit. I didn't even get an opportunity to contest like Ms. Carter said I would before she filled out the paperwork. I've been trying to get an appointment with the principal all week to no avail.

"I thought I would have an opportunity to state my case," I say, handing the file back to Ms. Toni. "Did Ms. Carter also tell you that Ellen got to go home for weeks to visit her family?"

"Yes, she did, but she says that Ellen's trip was planned and therefore excusable. You, on the other hand, simply disappeared."

"But my grandmother called the school explaining my absence. Mrs. Malone even sent home the rest of the writing work for me to complete at home so I'm sure Ms. Carter was aware of my unforeseen illness," as Mama called it when she informed the main office.

"You weren't sick for that long and Ms. Carter knows it," Ms. Toni says, smiling at me.

"How does she know anything other than what my grandmother told her?"

"Apparently, Misty and a few of the cheerleaders are friendly and she informed them about your necessity for a vacation, as she put it."

Misty. I should've known that heffa had something to do with this. Why would I get to start the year off drama free? Because of Misty's mischief last year, I was approached by my ex-boyfriend KJ's tramp of the week before I could even get off the bus, now this bull. I should've kicked her ass when I had the chance.

"Ms. Toni, Misty can't be taken seriously nor can she account for my whereabouts at any time."

"Well dear, unfortunately she can in this instance because she's your neighbor and that's as good as a witness on the stand. She's willing to put it in writing and everything."

What a bitch.

"This is unbelievable. How did Misty get so much clout around here?"

"When it comes to someone wanting you out they'll go through any extreme to get it done. And in this case, Ellen wants to be the uncontested star of cheer. Unfortunately, you're a threat. Also, if you're out, Misty's in by way of default because she was only cut because you scored higher than her. They need an even number of cheerleaders and she's waiting to take your place."

"That's way too much to think about right now." Why does Misty always want what I have?

"Well, you need to think about it because on top of it all is your true address. Yes, Misty's involved in that one, too. Her mom works in the attendance office. Don't think that girl's not up to more evil than good when it comes to you, Jayd. You've got to preempt her attacks or you'll never survive."

Ms. Toni sounds more like Mama than herself. No matter where the information's coming from I'm glad it's coming. I needed to be reminded to take care of my own back because I have real enemies with Misty being at the top of that list with a butcher knife.

The bell for fourth period rings loudly in the room.

"I don't know what else to say."

"Jayd, I know it seems like you always have battles to fight, and I'd like to tell you it's going to get easier, but I don't want to lie," Ms. Toni says, standing in front of me. "For queens, life is always a challenge. The day I met you two years ago I knew you were special. And believe me, honey, so does everyone else, which is why you need to take care of yourself." She wraps her thin arms around me hugging me tightly and I return the love.

"I know you're right. But I'm getting too tired to care." I want to cry, but I can't force the tears.

"Oh Jayd, never that. You can never retreat when in battle, my dear. You've got too much work to do. Remember your ancestors as well as the other women you represent. You've got to take care of you, forget about your little girl frenemies. They're merely a stepping stone to your success."

I pull away from Ms. Toni and grab my bags ready to head to Speech class. "So what should I do about cheer and my address?"

"As far as cheer goes, you need to get your story straight and quickly if you plan on contesting the claim. It also wouldn't hurt if you could get your grandmother up here to reiterate her written statement. As for the address, your mother's going to have to come in and sign her original affidavit and show proof of residency soon."

"Getting either of my mothers up here is easier said than done." I already know Mama's not going for it. She didn't want me in cheer in the first place. "But I'll see what I can do about it."

"Good, Jayd. And honestly, I think you're better off focusing on your other extracurricular activities as well as your schoolwork. If you're worried about your college applications, I can write you a gleaming letter of recommendation mentioning your brief, but successful time on the squad. And if Mr. Adelizi has a problem with that you tell him to come see me."

"What would I do without you in my corner?" I ask, reaching up to hug my school mama one more time before leaving her office.

"You would take care of yourself like only you can, but let's not think of such unpleasantries." Ms. Toni releases me from our embrace and signs my hall pass.

Something about her answer makes me uncomfortable, but I'll investigate that later as well as get to work on her antismoke potion. I'm still trying to figure out which form will work best: tincture, spray or herb bag. Maybe I can even bake her some sweet treats to help eliminate the craving for good. Maybe Mr. Adewale can help me figure some of this madness out, too.

"It's nice to see you this morning, Miss Jackson," Mr. Adewale says as I enter the full classroom. He's already calling roll and everyone's got his or her textbooks out ready to get fourth period under way.

"Hi, Mr. A," I say, passing him the note before walking to my desk in the front of the classroom. I nod "what up" to the rest of my crew before placing the heavy backpack down and taking my seat. This is one of the only classes most of us look forward to all day, if for no other reason most of the black and Latino student population's up in here. The class is basically an introduction to the African Student Union's meetings Mr. Adewale sponsors in his room twice per month. We have our first official ASU meeting of the new school year next week before the big membership rush begins. All loyalties should be solid by Homecoming, the first big event and the vote of the year. We've got to get more dedicated members on our team if we're going to have any significant impact on this school's social and political agenda.

I've got a busy day ahead of me, mostly copying my English reading in the library since Mrs. Bennett's textbooks have yet to arrive. She decided to make our first assignment due Friday, damn the books. She could give a damn about winning her students over as friends. I wish I had her cold attitude when it comes to certain people in my life, like Misty and Cameron, who are both missing from class today. They can run, but they can't hide. They have both gone out of their way to make my life more inconvenient than necessary. After I handle my urgent school business, I'm going to figure out a way to dismiss them permanently out of my circle of friends and enemies alike.

~ 8 ~
Unfriend

The ups and downs, the carousel/
People make the world go round.

—THE STYLISTICS

This week has been an emotional roller coaster, and I'm glad it's Friday so I can get off of it. Chance informed me that his mother's strongly requesting my presence sooner than later. After she came to me in my dream last night, I decided to join Chance at home this afternoon. I'm getting used to Alia being in the picture; she's coming too. It's weird coming home with Chance and his girlfriend when she's not Nellie. Nellie would love for me to unfriend Chance out of loyalty to her, but I can't do that. Chance and I have been drama partners and best friends for my entire time at Drama High and I love him like a brother. Besides, she screwed this relationship up not him.

The link between my spiritual clients and me is permanent until I do a series of cleansings to get their energy out of my head. When I began helping Mrs. Carmichael I noticed she could psychically call me through my dreams when she needed me. I'm developing the skill to receive my dream requests more regularly and to send out requests, too like a message on Facebook. I can post it out in the dream world and whoever wants to respond can. Mrs. Carmichael would be first on that list, no doubt.

I can't stay for long because I have a lot of work to do, but I can give Mrs. Carmichael an hour of my time. After that, I'm out no matter what type of liquor-induced hell she's going through. Hopefully she's been spraying the clarity mist I made for her on her body and around her home regularly. I think the first problems we need to address are her alcohol and nicotine addictions, then we can handle her other issues.

When we arrive at the Carmichael's mini Palos Verdes mansion, a huge, white van with a key logo is parked in the driveway, forcing both Chance and me to park on the street, which I don't mind. The hills are a bit difficult to balance my clutch on, but I'm becoming somewhat of an expert navigating the stick shift on the varied terrain in the South Bay.

We exit our separate vehicles and walk up the brick path toward the front porch passing up several piles of men's clothing stacked on the lawn. The antique oak and glass front door is wide open and we can see his mother inside pacing between the kitchen and the foyer, wineglass in hand. I can see I have some serious work to do. Mama always says voodoo isn't magic and this type of healing is obviously going to take some time.

"Mom, what's wrong with the front door? And why is all of dad's stuff on the front lawn?" Chance asks, passing up the man working on the massive door. I can't imagine anyone kicking that heavy thing in like doors in the hood suffer from time to time.

"Hello, girls, baby." Mrs. Carmichael blows her son a kiss without stopping her quick steps. "I'm divorcing your father," she says, throwing more Louis Vuitton luggage out the front door. If Nellie were here she'd gladly take those off Mrs. Carmichael's hands.

The locksmith looks like he wants to comment, but checks himself and continues his work in silence. It looks like Mrs. Carmichael's seen *Waiting to Exhale* one too many times. And from the crazy look in her eyes she just might set her husband's shit on fire, while she's tossing it.

"Mom, you always say that. But this is the first time you've gone after his stuff." Chance looks out the door at the luggage on the otherwise immaculate lawn and shakes his head.

"His secretary informed me of her impending maternity leave. The bitch has been single since she started working for your father three years ago." Mrs. Carmichael crosses the foyer and heads to the dining room where the bar is housed. I guess she needs something stronger. "The bastard didn't even want children and now he's going to be a father all over again."

"Mom, you don't need him. I'm here for you." Chance takes the whiskey bottle from his mother who begins to cry. Every time I come over here it's some heavy shit to deal with. Where's that spray when we need it?

Speechless, Alia grabs the roll of paper towels off the counter and passes them to Mrs. Carmichael who smiles at her. Nellie never got a genuine smile out of Chance's mom.

"Thank you, Alia." Mrs. Carmichael takes a sheet and loudly blows her nose.

"Mrs. Carmichael, here are your new keys. I'm all finished. The alarm company should be out soon to reset your code and password."

Whatever he was thinking before the full confession has changed his expression from one of judgment to sympathy.

"I'll take those, man," Chance says, walking over to the locksmith and signing the bill. He takes the new keys and places them on the table in the center of the foyer.

"Chance, I'm glad you finally saw through that gold-digging hussie you had the nerve to bring home. If you and Jayd can't be together I think Alia's a good choice."

We look shocked at her candor, but I'll blame it on the alcohol and think nothing of it. Alia's blushing, but says nothing and Chance simply shakes his head, used to his mother's ways.

"I think it's time to get you upstairs, Mom. I'll handle your husband if he comes home."

Chance has forgiven his mom for keeping his adoption a secret, but his dad has never been one of his favorite people. And now that Mr. Carmichael's been caught cheating on his mom all ties he ever had to the man are severed.

"We need to get away, Chance. I'm thinking Paris is nice this time of year. Yes, Europe since we weren't able to travel together this summer," Mrs. Carmichael says as Chance helps her upstairs.

"Wherever you want to go, Mom. But first let's get you to go to sleep, then we'll plan a trip." Chance looks back at us and smiles, directing us to go into the living room and wait. I have to be at work in an hour. I should hit the road soon since I'm not needed here any longer. Alia and Chance can get their Friday night started early without a third wheel slowing them down. I used to get excited about Jeremy and me spending our weekends together so I know how they feel. I miss having my man around.

"And Jayd, how is Jeremy?" Mrs. Carmichael asks from the top of the stairs. "I heard the London trip was fabulous this year."

"I guess it depends on who you talk to," I say, not wanting to get into that conversation again. I need to figure out a way to make liquor less of Mrs. Carmichael's friend and her good judgment more, soon. "Chance, I've got to get going or I'll be late to the shop."

"All right, Jayd. I'll see you at the party tomorrow," Chance says from his mother's room. I look at Alia who looks happy to see me go. This girl got everything she wanted and didn't have to be evil to get it. Every female I know needs to take lessons from her playbook.

"Bye, Mrs. Carmichael. See you later, Alia." Unlocking the front door is a bit more of a hassle with the extra bolt at the top. Short of using a sledgehammer there's no way Mr. Carmichael's getting through this thing. When love goes bad it can be the most vindictive time in a person's life. I pity Mr. Carmichael for betraying his wife. God doesn't like ugly and this is as unpleasant as it gets.

Last night was the busiest we've been at Netta's shop in months. Whatever Mama and Netta cleansed the space with after Netta's sisters left worked and brought prosperity back in full effect. Some of the positive vibes trickled down into my own work. I had no shortage of clients today. I even had to turn down some heads so I could help out with Nellie and Mickey's birthday housewarming party. I hope this party turns out better than Mickey's baby shower we held at Nigel's house. That event went from chill to hood in a matter of seconds and the same thing's liable to happen if any of Mickey's folks show up.

"Mickey, did we get a final RSVP head count? I need to know how many party favors to put out," Nellie says, in full Martha Stewart mode.

"I thought the point of having a party was to get gifts, not give them." Mickey's not into the good hostess act one bit. Nellie's had to compromise a lot for this joint venture, right down to the menu.

"That's how we get good gifts and more gracious guests."

Nellie continues tying ribbons on the tiny gift bags with all kinds of goodies inside. My girl knows how to throw a classy affair.

"Fine," Mickey says, sitting down at Rah's desk. "I'm going to see if we had any responses on Facebook and Twitter. I put out the word about an hour ago."

"You're just now inviting people to our party?" Nellie asks, mortified. "Who the hell's going to show up with hardly any notice? This is horrible, Mickey."

"Aren't you overreacting?" Mickey asks, unmoved by Nellie's usual antics. "If people want to roll through they will, no matter when they found out about the damned thing."

Furious, Nellie begins putting the small gold gift bags back in the box where she's keeping them. "There's no point in making any more of these. It's only going to be us at the party anyway. Some birthday."

Placing the last bag inside, Nellie picks up the box and storms out of the den, almost knocking Nigel down in the doorway.

"What did I miss?"

"Nothing important," I say, placing the last black napkin in the designated gold basket per Nellie's instructions. We're setting up the food and drinks on the back deck. Rah and Nigel have been cleaning the yard all day while us girls have been handling the inside. I've only been here for two hours and have done more than Mickey has all day. I understand Nellie's frustration, but I think it's time to settle down and eat. Whether or not anyone else shows up isn't my concern.

"Nigel, who the hell is Monica on your Facebook page?" Mickey asks, fully enraged. What the hell is on that computer?

"I don't know," Nigel says, lying across the futon. "You're the one checking the account."

"Well she poked your ass," Mickey says, pointing at the screen. "Strangers don't usually do that shit."

Mickey turns the screen toward Nigel who ignores her attitude. She's always tripping off who sends him messages on and off the Internet. I just recently set up my online profile, but there's nothing much on it yet. I put up a couple of pictures and that's it.

"I knew setting up that damned chat page was a mistake," Nigel says, tired from his manual work and Mickey's nagging. "I'm taking a nap before people start showing up."

"Well, I'm changing your relationship status to married," Mickey says, going into his settings. "Next time the ho wants to poke someone she can holla at me."

"Mickey, I don't want my business all out in the streets," Nigel says, throwing a pillow at her.

"Whatever, punk," she says, throwing it back. Sparring is part of their foreplay. I'd better make myself scarce if this turns into a full-on session between the two of them.

"Mickey, we aren't married yet," Nigel says, stepping behind Mickey. "What the hell?"

"We're close enough now that we share an address and a bed." Common Law isn't legal anymore, but I'm not getting in the middle of this one.

"Yeah, we do share a bed, don't we?" Nigel says, kissing Mickey's neck, distracting her the best way he knows how. My boy is as slick as they come, but Mickey's slicker. She may not change his status now, but she won't forget.

"I'll give y'all some privacy," I say, taking the party goods out with me. We need a "do not disturb" sign for the doors in this house. I hope they don't miss their own party fooling around. Nellie's in the guest bathroom getting dressed. I'm good in my jeans and off the shoulder orange top, courtesy of my mom's closet. Rah's putting the girls down in Nigel and Mickey's room. It's after nine. If people are coming they should be arriving shortly. It may be a Saturday night, but I have to work in the morning. I want to hang, but I can't be out too late. Friends or not, I can't let anyone mess with my money.

After a half hour of peace, Mickey, Nigel, and Rah emerge ready to hang. Nellie's finally finished putting herself together looking every bit the young diva she is. The birthday girls are in the same jumpsuit, but Nellie's is black while Mickey's wearing gold. They picked the colors and the outfits together. They've always liked dressing together for special occasions while I always prefer the individual route.

"Let the party begin," Mickey says, ready to get her birthday groove on. Nellie turns her nose up at the loud rap music blaring through the speakers, but changes her attitude when cars begin pulling in the driveway.

"David's here," Nellie says, running out the front door. David pulls up in his white Ford Focus, and Chance pulls up next parking his decked-out Chevy Nova. I don't know if money matters, but in this case, Chance is definitely the baller.

Nellie's new man exits his virgin mobile happy to see our girl. We all look at her like she's lost her mind, bringing dude to the party knowing Chance would be here. But Chance has a guest of his own.

"What's up, peeps?" Chance asks, opening the passenger door to let his companion out. Alia's beaming ear to ear minus the platinum across her teeth she's been sporting for the past two years.

"Alia, your braces are gone," I say, meeting them at the end of the driveway. I give them each a hug and look more closely at Alia's bright smile. She looks like a completely different person and her confidence shows she feels like one, too.

"Yeah. Isn't it great? And right in time for senior pictures, too," she says, showing off her pearly whites for all to see. I'm happy for her. She's a pretty girl and it's time she thought so. And if any dude can make a girl feel her best it's Chance. He'll spoil her like no other—a fact Nellie certainly misses because David's supposedly humble ass is far from rolling like her ex.

"Hey, everyone," Nellie says, joining us. "This is my friend, David. David, these are my friends Jayd, Mickey, and Nigel."

Chance looks at Nellie, waiting for his and Alia's names to be called, which Nellie never does. Even if they're not together anymore Chance and Nellie can be friends if they're mature about it. Nellie doesn't feel the same way.

"Oh, so it's like that?" Chance says, taking Alia by the hand and holding it tight. "What's up, man? I'm Chance and this is my girl, Alia," Chance says, wiping the plastered smile right off Nellie's face. That's what she gets for being rude.

"Your girl?" Nellie asks. Alia's been feeling Chance since they went to elementary school together and she wasted no time making her move once he was free and interested. Good for her. Hopefully she'll appreciate Chance's good heart. They both deserve it.

"What's hood, my nigga?" Chance says, giving Nigel dap. Rah looks like he wants to hit Chance for his greeting.

"Too soon, man. Too soon," Nigel says, correcting our boy. Chance's newfound blackness is taking some getting used to and Rah is less than sympathetic to the transformation.

"My bad, my brotha," Chance says. "Where's the gift table, man? Me and Alia got y'all something real classy."

"I'll show you," Mickey says, suddenly interested in the gifts. Whatever Chance bought is bound to be expensive.

Nellie takes David around the back where the food's waiting to be devoured. I think it's time for me to head to the deck area with my girl and her plain-looking dude. I'll give David a shot for Nellie's sake even if my gut tells me he's a snake.

"Chance can't come up in here fronting, Nigel," Rah says. "We've got too many real niggas from the hood coming tonight."

"I got him, man," Nigel says. "Chance is a little confused, but he's harmless. Now that nigga David, I'm not sure about."

"So it's not just me who doesn't like that fool," I say, shrugging Rah in the side. Nigel and Rah nod in agreement. Both of my boys follow me to the back of the house. Chance has already got the session started sharing a fat blunt with Mickey. Whatever doubt Rah had about Chance's sincerity vanished with the presence of good herb.

"We haven't smelled that kind of good shit in a min," Nigel says, stepping into the rotation. Nellie and David are sitting in a corner across the yard in their own little world. They can stay there as far as we're concerned.

Rah and Nigel's supply's dwindled due to Rah's disagreement with Lance over Sandy's ass. They've decided it's best not to do business with Lance until that mess is straightened out, mostly because Sandy's ass can't be trusted.

"I got y'all any time you need it, man. My boy grows the best shit in his closet." Chance takes another hit and passes it to Alia and then Rah who's impressed by Chance's rolling technique.

"In his closet? That's what I'm talking about," Nigel says, coughing out smoke. Mickey pats his chest like the true ride or die chick she is for her boo. They may not be the perfect couple, but I can't imagine two people more suited for each other. I used to think me and Jeremy had that kind of link, but after Cameron's revelation I'm not so sure.

"Open my gift," Chance says, instantly sparking Nellie's interest who comes over to see what's in the big box. "It'll break the ice."

"Cool," Mickey says, retrieving the present from the table next to the sliding glass doors leading back into the den. Nellie helps Mickey rip the wrapping paper off, but it's not what they expected. "It's a game," Mickey says, disappointed.

"A stupid game is your version of a classy gift?" Nellie's just as ungrateful as Mickey. If I were Chance I'd never buy them another thing. I gave them money because that's their favorite gift of all and they could both use it. Neither of them have a job.

"Yeah," Chance says, smiling at Alia whose eyes are as red as her boyfriend's. "I didn't know what to buy for a house-warming-slash-birthday party, so I thought a game was appropriate for both events." Chance smiles big, proud of his clever thought process. I think it's a good compromise.

"And there's a Target gift certificate inside the card," Alia adds. "That was my idea."

"Now you're talking," Mickey says, opening the card without reading it. "A hundred dollars! Thank you, man." Mickey kisses Chance on the cheek and hugs Alia, officially welcoming her to the crew.

Nellie's jealousy takes the best of her and she goes back to join her man who's on the phone ignoring us all. I'm not sure if anyone else will show up. Nellie's right about our girl's procrastination. Leaving Mickey in charge of contacting the guests was a mistake.

"Let's play," Alia says, opening the box. "I love Truth or Dare."

"I don't," I say, reliving bad memories of many arguments over the game. "Someone always ends up getting hurt. We should watch a movie since it looks like it's just us for the night."

There's enough food and drinks on the table to feed an army. In another fifteen minutes or so the munchies will kick in for most of the crew taking care of half of the waffles, chicken wings, and appetizers from Roscoe's. The rest can go in the empty fridge at my mom's apartment.

"I'm going to go take a leak," Nigel says, walking into the den. "I'm with the game when I get back."

Alia sets the game up, against my better judgment, while the rest of us get something to eat. We start the game when Nigel returns, but there's something different about his demeanor. He was gone for longer than I know it takes for any dude to pee. Whatever he had going on in the house has put him in a foul mood.

"Truth or dare, Jayd," Nigel says, snatching up a card and scaring the shit out of me. My friends know I hate this game and I'm pissed I was outnumbered yet again for this evening's entertainment. Who gets tired of watching movies?

"Truth, fool," I answer, popping another chip in my mouth. Maybe I'll choke and get out of playing this godforsaken game.

"Is Mickey talking to her ex again?" Nigel did not just ask me that shit in the context of a stupid game and in front of Mickey, too. He knows I can't lie to him but I also can't rat out my girl.

"Nigel, where'd that come from?" Mickey asks, looking as guilty as she is. I told her she should've told Nigel when her ex first contacted her no matter if we were able to take care of the problem for the time being or not. The truth always has a way of coming out.

I look around the dimly lit porch, the slow baseline in the background providing a countdown for my impending confession.

"Come with it, Jayd," Rah says, butting in. He's always liked torturing me. "Yes or no?"

"I pass," opting out of the ugly scenario. There's more going on here than a simple game.

Mickey breathes a sigh of relief, but she knows her ass is on the line.

"You can't pass, Jayd. It's Truth or Dare. Not Truth, Dare or Pass." Nigel's hard-core when it comes to competition, making him an excellent athlete and a ruthless friend. He knows I'm holding back, but how does he know?

"Nigel, what the hell kind of question is that? Isn't it supposed to be relevant to my life, not some dumb shit I don't want to be involved in?" Now I know he knows I'm covering up for my girl, but I'm not saying another word about it. This is between the two of them.

"Omission is as good as a yes." Nigel stands up and glares at his woman hard who's sitting in a chair next to Chance and Alia. If Alia's going to hang out in our territory she'll have to get used to how we roll.

"Hey man, we're supposed to be playing a game and enjoying ourselves, remember?" Rah says, standing next to his boy who towers over Mickey.

Mickey looks from her man to Rah, scared of Nigel's next move. I'm a bit nervous, too. Nigel takes betrayal very seriously.

"I knocked over the pile of mail from my mom's house on my way to the bathroom and noticed a strange letter," Nigel says, taking an envelope from his pocket and unfolding it. The address is written in the same red ink Mickey's letters are written in. "Imagine my surprise when it was a letter congratulating me and Mickey on moving in together and for Nickey's birth. My first thought was how did this nigga get my address, but then I remembered his homies and your little brother coming to the baby shower." Nigel tosses the letter at Mickey who looks shocked by Nigel's attitude. "My next thought was how did he know about me and you moving to Rah's?"

"Nigel, it's not like that," Mickey begins, but Nigel's not having it.

"He had the nerve to tell me he's getting out on parole for good behavior. The letter's dated three days ago, Mickey. When were you going to tell me about him being out?" Nigel's yelling loudly over the music causing Nellie and David to look up from their deep conversation.

"I didn't know the fool was out of jail, Nigel. I swear," Mickey says, pleading with her man to understand. She stands up in an effort to hug Nigel, but he's inconsolable.

"Who'd let a convicted murderer out after only serving a minimal amount of his fifteen years?" Alia asks, innocent to our reality.

"That's what happens when a brother kills another brother, especially if they're gang members," Rah says, matter-of-factly. "The jails are overcrowded and as the system sees it, their work was done for them without getting their hands dirty. It's a win-win situation."

I know Rah's thinking about his own dad who's been locked up in Atlanta for years with no chance of parole anytime soon. The drug laws between crack and pure cocaine are biased, with the latter having less time attached to it because those dealers are usually white, upper-class dudes as opposed to the crack dealers in the hood. If Tre were some preppy white dude from Redondo they'd put Mickey's ex-man under the jail and forget all about him. He must've had one hell of an attorney to get him probation his first time up.

"Don't try to clean it up. I know he couldn't wait to contact you once he got out, ain't that right, girl?"

Mickey looks like a deer caught in headlights. Lucky for her Nickey starts screaming right in time to save her mama, but only for a while. Nigel's no fool. He's going to find out they've been in contact and when he does, the shit's going to hit the fan. This wasn't the type of party Mickey and Nellie had in mind at all. Instead of good gifts and a crowd of people, they both received the opposite. It looks like me and my girls are going to be three single black females if shit doesn't start going our way.

~ 9 ~
Single Black Female

You got spark, you, you got spunk/
You, you got something all the girls want.

—NICKI MINAJ

After yesterday's party Nigel, Mickey, and Rah are in recovery mode. We haven't heard from Nellie since she left with David after Nigel's exposé. Nigel smoked himself to sleep and Rah and Chance accompanied him. Alia and I stayed up talking for a while before we finally passed out. When I woke up on Rah's couch this morning everyone was still asleep, a luxury I rarely have. I worked all day and finished my English assignment due in the morning.

Sometimes I feel like I'm the only one of my friends who takes schoolwork seriously. They never talk about doing homework on the weekends. It gets on my nerves I have more to do than them, but I'm trying to check the hater in me. I've decided to take my goddaughters to visit Dr. Whitmore with me and give their parents time to recuperate fully from our late night. Then we get to go back to Rah's and eat leftovers.

As we exit the car I have a strange feeling someone's watching me. I look around the quiet street noticing the City of Compton sign in the center divider where the airport is located. I shake off the feeling, put Nickey in her stroller and take Rahima's hand and head toward the small office. Dr.

Whitmore should be there even on Sunday. Holy day or not, the good doctor has work to do.

My uncle Bryan doesn't work on Sundays due to his busy deejaying schedule on the weekends. Otherwise I'd walk down to the opposite end of Alondra Boulevard where Miracle Market is located and hit him up for a few free snacks for my babies and me. It's just as well, the last thing I want to deal with today is fools asking me for some spare change when I know where them and their baby mamas live. A few of my uncles—Kurtis included—could be out there, too, and they're the last fools I want to run into.

I step onto the sidewalk pushing the stroller ahead of me and again feel all eyes are on me, but whose?

"I'm bugging, huh, girls?" I say to my goddaughters who both look up at me like I'm speaking German, but I know what I feel. And unlike my crew, I haven't been smoking or drinking a thing to get my senses way off like this.

"Auntie Jayd, doggy," Rahima says, pointing toward the building where Dr. Whitmore's office sits.

I notice the brown pit bull in front of the office door. Two more dogs join him to form a pack. What the hell?

"Pet doggy?" Rahima asks, unaware of the impending danger we're in. I would scream, but that'll only make it worse. I haven't had to fight off dogs in a while but it's an experience I'll never forget. If I were by myself I'd simply run back to the car, but I can't move that fast with two babies to care for.

"No, baby," I say, protectively shielding Rahima with my left arm while moving the stroller behind me. "These are not nice dogs."

Rahima, sensing my fear, moves behind me without another word. The dogs snarl at me as I slowly walk backward, looking down the entire time. Then, without warning, the lead pit barks at us loudly while the others growl in unison.

"Shit," I say under my breath. I would be caught out here alone with Nickey and Rahima. Where's my backup when I need it? I look at the dogs slowly walking toward us, scared for my girls. Rahima begins to cry and I don't blame her. I would, too, if I weren't busy plotting our next move.

I spot a brick on the curb next to us and pick it up ready to defend my girls. The first one looks me dead in the eye and I notice his cold blue stare has a familiar feeling—Esmeralda. I know she's a bitch, but I didn't know she could literally become one.

"You know what you have to do, Jayd. Use my powers to take control of hers," my mom says, on cue as always. *"Don't let your fear overcome you. You can do this."*

"Okay," I say aloud, unable to speak to her telepathically at the moment. The only things I can focus on are the angry dogs coming at us and how to cool their thoughts before they move in for the kill.

"Auntie Jayd," Rahima whines, tugging on my pant leg. Poor baby. Even Nickey begins to moan in the midst of the moment. I'll be damned if I let Esmeralda intimidate us. I don't care what shape she takes on. I whipped her ass when she decided to come at me in the form of a crow the night of my initiation and I'm going to fix her ass good now, too.

"Stay here, baby. Auntie's got this," I say, patting Rahima's hand and placing it beside her. I take three steps closer to the dogs holding their ground in front of Dr. Whitmore's office. They're obviously attempting to keep us from going inside, but they're the ones who need to surrender. I might be by myself with two dependents, but I'm never alone.

"Your tricks don't scare me, Esmeralda," I say, staring the largest canine in the eye, feeling the blank stare move from its head to mine. It's definitely under Esmeralda's influence. I can feel the pounding in the dog's head as it tries to grapple with it's own thoughts.

All three dogs begin barking loudly, causing my girls to scream in horror. Then, they approach. I have no choice but to fling the brick as hard as I can. It hits the smallest dog and he's down. The others, unphased by the assault on their companion, continue to charge across the small street separating us from them. I continue to stare down the alpha dog, causing her to stop and squirm from the pain I'm redirecting toward her thanks to Maman's power present in my own. I hate to hurt an animal, but I'll be damned if they get any closer.

"Jayd," Dr. Whitmore calls from his front door.

The third dog halts noticing he's not only alone, but outnumbered. With his two mates down he runs away, which saves me from having to mentally cripple his ass, too.

I turn around and run toward my goddaughters who are no longer crying, but still stunned at what just happened. I hug them both tightly reassuring them that everything's okay.

"The mean doggies went bye-bye." Rahima wipes her wet eyes and looks over her shoulder to make sure they're gone.

"What happened?" Dr. Whitmore says, coming to my aid. If he hadn't come out when he did who knows how it would've ended.

"Esmeralda and more of her tricks, that's what," I say, following Dr. Whitmore into his office.

"I curse the day that woman was born," Dr. Whitmore says, slamming the door behind us. "She'll never give up on this revenge endeavor against your grandmother and her lineage. It's unfortunate some people don't know when to quit."

"I hear you, Dr. Whitmore."

I take Nickey out of her stroller and hug her, also checking her diaper. She doesn't need changing yet, but I like to keep an eye on her diaper rash, which is all but gone thanks to

Mama's special balm. It was so bad a month ago looking at her red skin brought tears to my eyes. But Mickey seems to be on top of her new mommy duties now, thanks in large part to Dr. Whitmore.

"How are you doing since your initiation, little Jayd?" he says, shining a light in my eyes and forcing my tongue out. "From the looks of the way you handled that situation, you're getting the hang of your developing powers, or so it would seem."

"I'm sleeping well, if that's what you mean." The girls watch quietly while the good doc does his job.

"Good sleep is essential, but how are you handling stress? Even at your young age it can be crippling." Dr. Whitmore looks in my ears and up my nose. This invasive visit is causing me to feel stress. "Did you finish the herbs I prescribed?"

"Yes sir, I did. Every last bit." And they were horrible but I'll keep that part to myself.

"Good. Now on to round two," he says, opening the large cabinet full of numerous concoctions from God knows where. I looked in one of the bags Mama had to boil before I could take them and could've sworn I saw a spider's carcass.

"Seriously? Now what's wrong with me?" I don't know how much more of this alternative medicine I can stomach.

"On the contrary, Jayd. Everything's going well." That's good to know, but little consolation when he's putting more horse pills in a bag for me to take home. "We just want to keep it that way, don't you agree?"

"Yes, I guess so." Nickey looks around at all of the Chinese writing on the walls. I feel as confused by the visit as she looks by the black characters.

"Well, you need to know it. You've got a lot riding on your spiritual, mental, and physical success, little lady, and the stronger you are the better you'll be able to handle it. You must continue to fortify your blood no matter how strong it may be." Dr. Whitmore looks down at the brass heart and cross emblem hanging at the end of my eleke.

"I got you, doc," I say, making him smile, but not laugh. I've never heard anything close to laughter come from him. Maybe Mama knows how to get a chuckle out of the stoic medicine man.

"It seems like a lot today, but tomorrow it will be a thing of the past," Dr. Whitmore says, passing me the white paper bag filled with bitter treats. "Trust me, you won't have to take herbs forever if you do it correctly the first time around."

"Will do."

"And there's a tincture for the baby's runny nose," he says, reminding me of the real reason I wanted to bring Nickey with me today. "You can tell her mother to give it to her three times a day before her meals. The mucus should disappear in a couple of days."

"Thank you, Dr. Whitmore, for everything." He always knows what to do even when I don't ask the question. In another time and place, Mama and him would have made a powerful couple. Maybe they did make one back in the day. It's just a feeling, but I think they had a relationship before Daddy came into the picture. Who knows how their destinies would have unfolded if things were different. I'm glad Dr. Whitmore's around when we need him. He's literally a lifesaver.

Dr. Whitmore's capsules are becoming easier to swallow making me grateful for the small things in life. After the day I've had I need a good night's sleep and for me that includes active dreaming. I hope Nickey and Rahima have sweet dreams and forget about the dog attack earlier this afternoon. Hopefully my dreams are peaceful and my sleep, solid. Monday morning will be here before I know it.

*   *   *

"Look at that beautiful neck—I mean skin. The gold chain against your copper skin is glowing, Queen Califia. Absolutely magnificent."

At first, my great ancestor is flattered by Cortes' compliment, knowing she is indeed one of the most beautiful women he's ever seen. But she also can see something else in his intentions: The foreigner wants her gold and her blood.

"Muchas gracias," she says, speaking Cortes' native tongue much to his surprise and pleasure. She can read him like a book, but not soon enough to see how this confrontation will end. Vanity was always the queen's Achilles' heel.

Cortes' men encircle Queen Califia and her female warriors, causing them to draw their swords ready to fight. The all male army looks at the women soldiers excited by their passion. Cortes and his men don't even have the good sense to feel threatened; pride was always their weakness.

"Por favor, senora. Put away your weapons and leave the bloodshed for another day and more even battle, shall we?"

"I don't see anything uneven about this battle, senor." Califia's warriors yell in agreement ready to throw down. Now I know where my fighting spirit comes from. Williams women never retreat in battle. "And it's senorita. Califia belongs to no man."

"Not for long," Cortes says, smiling cunningly. "If you'll agree to become my wife I will spare the lives of these women and your own."

My great-grandmother—several times over—looks at this white man like he's lost his mind. She could step on him if she wanted to. Califia stands about six feet tall while Cortes looks a good foot shorter.

"I'd rather die a single woman than live as your wife."

"I'm sorry to hear that," Cortes says. He looks Califia in

the eyes, smiling wide so she can't miss the fangs prevalent on either side of his mouth. "I'll see to it that your deaths are not without merit."

"Adios, mio," Califia says, not believing her eyes and our sight is rarely wrong.

"Your God can't help you now." Cortes gives his men the signal to charge, his entire army displaying their vampirish roots. Without preparation or warning Califia and her army is defenseless against the supernatural beings.

"You can't have my blood or my love, Cortes."

"Fine then. I'll just take your gold." Cortes advances toward Califia, reaching for her jewelry but he can't resist the pulsating veins in her neck. In one quick movement he's got his teeth in her flesh, causing the armies to go to war. With the chaos ensuing around them, Califia and Cortes are suspended in time while he drains the life out of my ancestor.

"No!" I scream out of my sleep. I smack the alarm clock on the coffee table next to my mom's couch silencing the loud beeping.

It's time to get up for school, but that's not what pulled me out of my sleep. It can't be a coincidence seeing vampires in my dreams and dealing with Misty's changes in reality. I touch my neck checking for bite marks. It wouldn't be the first time I woke up from one of my dreams with a souvenir. I'll talk to Mama about my dream later. We have work to do in the spirit room today after our clients leave. Vampires and ancient mothers in our bloodline isn't appropriate shoptalk for a busy Monday afternoon.

Today wasn't a bad day as far as Mondays go. I turned in my homework, talked to Mr. Adewale about the agenda for the ASU meeting later this week, and managed to make a decent week's worth of tips in a few hours. The only thing lingering is my ill dream from this morning. I beat Mama here from the shop. She refuses to ride in the car with me unless she has no choice. Once the shop is locked up Netta will drop her off. It's too late for her to walk home by herself.

Gunlock Avenue's quiet tonight. There are a few neighbors hanging, like Mr. Gatlin across the street outside watering his lawn, and the Webb brothers playing dominoes on their front porch, but mostly everyone else is in for the evening. I might as well make my way to the back house. I'm tired and need to get started on my homework or risk not doing it all. Hopefully Mama won't have me back here all night.

"Russell, get your ass in this house and stop snooping around outside," Esmeralda says from her front door, yelling at her new houseguest like he's a pet instead of her boyfriend. Mr. Gatlin looks across the street into Esmeralda's yard, longing for his former companion. I guess now that she's got a new man the old one's out.

Esmeralda's man is wearing a black hoodie and sweats reminding me of a bank robber. He looks real thuggish for an old dude. Noticing me in the driveway, Russell comes closer to my side of the split grassy area separating the two properties and sniffs my way. I don't need dog senses to smell the stale weed and beer stench he's sporting. I can't make out his eyes but his bushy, red beard and mustache and long yellow nails are impossible to miss.

"Russell, do as you're told." Esmeralda repeats the command, but Russell's infatuated with his latest prey—me.

Netta's reggae music gets here before she pulls into the driveway behind me, but Russell doesn't move an inch and neither do I for fear he loves to chase.

"Russell, inside, now," Esmeralda commands.

Russell grunts and obeys his master, running through the porch gate and into the confines of Esmeralda's home. Nothing about that encounter was normal.

"Jayd, are you okay? What are you doing out here alone?" Mama asks, exiting Netta's large pickup. Netta lowers the volume to hear for herself that I'm okay. She has to pick up her son from work across town; otherwise she'd accompany Mama inside.

"Yeah. Esmeralda was just walking her pet," I say, locking the car door behind me and helping Mama with her loot. We wave good night to Netta.

"If you talk to a man like he's a dog he'll act like one," Mama says, heading toward the spirit room with her heavy bags in tow. I close the dilapidated wooden gate behind me, ready to get on with this evening's festivities.

"I hear that, Mama." I should share that bit of wisdom with Mickey, not that she'll heed my advice. She and Nigel aren't on the best of terms and rather than sweet-talking him she's been giving him hella lip in return.

"Esmeralda's even given that old fool a new name: Russell. I don't know why. His name's Rousseau. Always has been and always will be no matter how much she denies it."

I take Mama's bags so she can find her keys to the small house. "I can tell that jackass anywhere when I see him. I don't remember much about him other than he was a fisherman in New Orleans and they dated briefly before he disappeared. I've got a bad vibe, especially with Esmeralda's growing influence in the community."

We settle into the warm space removing our shoes at the door. I place the bags in the main room and join Mama at the kitchen table for some tea.

"Mama, do you think vampires are real?" I ask, easing in to my dream. "I had a dream about Queen Califia getting the blood sucked out of her by a vampire version of Cortes." She dismissed Misty's teeth as a potion that will eventually wear off. But real vampires are something completely different.

"Jayd, we don't need real vampires in our neighborhood. We've got enough evil to deal with: drugs, poverty, and other bloodsuckers take the life out of our people and make them slaves until they die. Look at Pam. She was once a beautiful little girl, just like Rahima. One challenge after another beat that girl down to the point where she had no more fight left in her. Eventually, she just gave in."

"Yeah, Mama. But I mean white folks' vampires; I'm talking Twilight, Dracula, The Lost Boys, Buffy the Vampire Slayer and all." Mama looks at me and sees I'm really freaked out by my latest vision. Dealing with potions and sleepwalking episodes is one thing, supernatural beings trying to take a bite out of my ass is on another level.

"Well, Jayd, Mama Califia's gift of sight was to see the unseen. So if you saw a vampire then you have to trust your instinct. Maybe she's warning you to notice what's hidden in plain sight." Something about Russell gives me the feeling he's the one I'm being warned against.

"What else do you know about Esmeralda's new man?" I ask, sipping the hot tea Mama poured for us. From the ingredients in the bags we're making dinner for the orisha. As hungry as I am I might have to take a sample of the meal before we serve it to the shrine.

"I know he's a damn fool who should've stayed in whatever New Orleans gutter he crawled out of. His people are no good. Him and his younger brothers are heroin and crack dealers. His younger brothers picked rape and murder as their chosen professions. There's a thread of evil in his bloodline that goes back to their European predecessors."

"So vampires are real?" I ask. We both rise from the table and wash our hands in the kitchen sink ready to cook. Mama passes me the plastic bags full of groceries for washing. I miss being in the kitchen with Mama on a daily basis. There's nothing like her cooking or the knowledge she drops while throwing down. I take the green bell peppers from the strainer and begin chopping them on my mini cutting board and pass my grandmother the celery to prepare.

"Vampires are as real as zombies are in our culture, Jayd. There are many types of venomous, bloodsucking creatures in the world, not just the ones you see on television or read in a book. But really, who has time for that kind of shit?" Mama continues chopping the celery until she cuts into her own flesh. "Shit!"

Before the four letter word is fully out of her mouth, we hear Esmeralda's back door slam shut where we see her new dude's on the porch looking dead at Mama through the window.

"Mama, are you okay?" I ask without taking my eyes off of our audience. He's salivating; he wants to get over here so bad, but why?

"I'm fine, Jayd," Mama says, running her finger under the cold water from the faucet. "It's just a little knick."

We both continue looking at Esmeralda's man looking at us.

"What the hell is wrong with him?" I ask while passing Mama a bandage from the first aid kit under the sink.

"Like I said, Jayd, there are all types of vampires in the world. And some are attracted to very specific blood types. There are a few out there searching for Williams women blood and will try to get it any way they can."

"That's not good," I say, placing the bandage over Mama's wound. Russell goes back inside as quickly as he appeared. With the wound covered he's lost interest in our activity.

"No, it's not," Mama says, rubbing her sore finger. "But like everything else in life, there are the consequences that come with the blessings. Our enemies will live as long as we do. It's just a part of life, Jayd."

This is a whole new level of hating I'm not prepared for. Even with my ancestors in my corner vampires, shape-shifters, and anything else Esmeralda's got in her arsenal's starting to freak me way the hell out.

"I don't know how you've dealt with Esmeralda all these years." We resume our food preparation with caution.

"Real friends and family are essential for survival in this dog-eat-dog world we find ourselves in," Mama says, putting the chopped vegetables in a large glass bowl before moving on to the next task. "Speaking of friends, Dr. Whitmore told me you paid him a visit yesterday. Take his medicine and watch yourself when you're alone. Our enemies are waiting for a weak moment and we can't give it to them, child. Never turn your back on our enemies."

And enemies we have. It seems like that's all I've got these days. I know my crew are my best friends, but they always have so much drama going on in their own lives they're not much help to me. Sometimes I feel alone in this world with no one who truly understands what it is I go through on a daily basis. I'm trying not to get overwhelmed but the shit is hard. With haters on my ass at home and at school when can a girl catch a break?

The rest of the week has been rather uneventful, but it's kind of hard to beat all that went down last weekend. Mrs. Bennett made sure to remind me about my necessity to show proof of residency every damn day. My mom finally made the appointment for this morning without any notice. I'm grateful she fit my needs into her busy schedule but why did she have to wait until Friday to do it? I wanted one day of peace this week and sitting in the main office for any amount of time is the exact opposite of my wish.

* * *

"Come on, Jayd. Let's get this shit over with. I've got to get to work on time all week if I'm going to take next Friday off to go to Cabo with my boo," my mom says as she smoothes the form-fitting dress over her hips admiring her figure in the mirror attached to her closet door. My mom's been jogging overtime to get rid of the extra fifteen pounds she put on in the year she's been with Karl. He feeds her well and treats her even better. It must be nice to think the world revolves around your schedule.

"I heard that, young lady. Don't forget who you're talking to, verbally or not." My mom knows I'm telling the truth no matter how much it may hurt.

"Mom, why are you mad at me? It's not my fault you didn't get your mail," I say, pouting like a five-year-old.

My mom slits her emerald eyes at me and I know I've gone too far. As Mama likes to remind me every so often, no matter how old I get I don't have the right to talk back to my elders—even when I'm right.

"Watch it, little girl," my mom says, checking herself in the mirror one more time. Her low-cut, knee length dress shows just enough cleavage to incite the hater in others without going overboard. And her Steve Madden black pumps give the outfit just the right finishing touch to look professional, yet sexy.

"I'm sorry."

"I know I slipped, but Jayd, I'm going to need you to pick up my mail from now on. I don't have the time to call Mary and check on it and you know she's busy with all of those babies and what not."

The what not is her man being strung out on cocaine, stealing from their family business, and subsequently running off with the nanny. Mary and my mom have been tight for years, but because of all the unexpected drama, Mary fell off the radar and the mail went right along with it. But still, my mom should've kept on top of it. Then we wouldn't have to go into the main office this morning and deal with this bull. She knows they send her a new affidavit to sign every year and she has to show proof of residency just like everyone else. How could she forget when it's her only responsibility as far as my education is concerned?

"Never mind all that, Jayd," my mom says, grabbing her purse and unlocking the front door. "Let's go before traffic gets bad. That's your problem. You don't know when to let shit go."

Whether I let this go or not, she's still wrong, but at least she's handling her business now. Maybe I'll learn to let go when people learn to do what they're supposed to.

My mom parks Kurtis's Camry in front of the main office and I pull up behind her. Usually I'd park in the lot, but I don't want to risk making my mom wait while I find a spot. She's already irritated enough that she had to drive all the way to Redondo Beach early in the morning and I don't want to piss her off even more.

"I'm always amazed at how big this campus is," my mom says as she exits her vehicle. She's only been here three times, including this visit. I can see how my high school can be overwhelming.

"Me, too."

We lock our cars and head toward the front steps. My mom runs her hand over her smooth ponytail, adjusts the Gucci bag on her shoulder and opens one of the double doors to the main building.

"This way," I say, pointing toward my counselor's office. Mr. Adelizi's been waiting for me to take care of this since last week. Hopefully he's prepared and we can get on with this formality quickly.

"Good morning, Mr. Adelizi. This is my mother, Lynn Jackson," I say, introducing them before sitting in one of two chairs opposite his chair on the other side of the desk.

"So, you're Jayd's mother," Mr. Adelizi says, obviously enamored by my mom's beauty, as most men are. There's just something about Lynn Marie Williams-Jackson that stops dudes in their tracks. Before her engagement she was the hottest chick on the scene, with expensive gifts and stalkers alike. Now that my mom's nearly settled down, she's happier, but I know she still loves the attention.

"The one and only." My mom smiles at my counselor as he gestures for her to take a seat. "Here's my current proof of residency," my mom says, whipping out her car insurance bill and placing it on Mr. Adelizi's overwhelmed desk. "Where do I sign?" she asks, getting down to business. My mom has no time to waste, especially not on a homely white dude.

"I'll get the paperwork from the secretary. Wait right here," Mr. Adelizi says, stepping from behind the cluttered desk he's always buried beneath. On his way out he knocks over a cup of coffee setting on the bookshelf closest to the door, spilling it all over the place.

"Are you okay?" I ask, taking a few napkins off his desk and passing them to him. My mom tries to stifle her giggle, but it's no use. The embarrassment is written all over his face and his tie.

"Yes, I'm fine," Mr. Adelizi says, patting his clothing. "I'll be right back."

"So that's the guy in control of your college future? Great." My mom rolls her bright eyes and makes me laugh. Leave it to her to blame the victim.

"He's not as bad as he used to be," I say, feeling bad for the poor guy.

After a few moments, Mr. Adelizi reappears with the forms. "Just sign right there and here."

"Ms. Jackson. So you're single?" Mr. Adelizi asks, noticing my mom's signature.

"Not for long," she says, showing off her emerald and diamond ring.

If I didn't know better I'd say Mr. Adelizi was disappointed. He's got jungle fever bad. I didn't even know he liked black women.

"Neither did he," my mom says so only the two of us can hear.

"Well, I think that's it. Thank you for coming in, Ms. Jackson." Mr. Adelizi checks over the papers while my mom and I get up ready to roll. My mom wants to get her day started and I want to get mine over.

"You're welcome, and hopefully I won't have to see you again until my baby graduates in June." My mom shakes Mr. Adelizi's hand and exits the cramped space. My mom's time is valuable and she has no problem letting everyone who has the pleasure of interacting with her know it.

"Yes, but if you need anything don't hesitate to call." Mr. Adelizi reaches into his wet shirt pocket and hands my mom a coffee-stained business card.

"I'll do that." My mom politely takes the damp card and exits his office behind me. I wave to my counselor anxious to get on with this Friday. I have much work to do at Netta's after school. There's much money to be made this weekend and shopping to do. Now that my ends are stacking steadily I again can take time Saturday to revamp my closet full of new colorful clothing before studying for the rest of the night. This year has started with a bang both academically and socially. Maybe it's just me, but so far senior year hasn't been as great as people make it out to be.

"Thanks, Mom," I say, giving her a hug. I'm glad she accompanied me to school this morning no matter how brief her visit has been. I miss hanging with my mommy.

"No problem, baby. I'll see you later." Later when? The only time I see my mom is when she drops by her apartment to stock up on clean clothes because she's run out at Karl's house. And with Jeremy and I not speaking, her small crib has been especially lonely.

"Jayd, Ms. Jackson," Jeremy says, almost running straight into us as he approaches the main office from the front door, late as usual. I want to tell him that I was just thinking about him, but words don't flow as easily as they used to between us.

"Hey, Jeremy," my mom says, passing him by and forcing me to do the same. I want to reach out to him, but I know it's not the right time.

"Nice charm," Jeremy says, commenting on my veve. The golden crossed-out heart illuminates off my white blouse making it hard to miss. "It kind of looks like a broken heart, doesn't it?" Jeremy's blue eyes are riddled with pain. I feel him; my heart's broken, too. Jeremy looks away and continues his sprint toward first period.

A broken heart is a good way to describe life in general, especially life in high school. Everyone I know has drama in and out of his or her love lives. It sucks when a good thing is gone; it's as simple as that. But if the end is a part of life why does it have to hurt so much?

"You're really jaded by this little white boy, aren't you, Jayd?" my mom says, opening the double doors and leading the way down the few steps to her car. My mom just doesn't get it.

"I just want to be normal and to have a normal, happy senior year of high school. Is that too much to ask?" I lean up against the Camry watching my mom walk around to the driver's side.

"Hell yes, it's too much to ask, girl. You have the visual powers of all the women who came before you and it's an amazing blessing," she says, unlocking the door and getting in. My mom starts the car and rolls down the front windows so we can wrap our conversation up in person, not that we need to. We can speak mind to mind no matter where we are. "Being normal is completely out of the question."

I bend down over the passenger's side window to make eye contact with my mom so she can really vibe off what I'm feeling. "Sometimes I just wish I could walk around school invisible. I wish no one knew my name, I wish I didn't have to speak out in class or deal with Misty's evil ass. I just want to know what it's like to not have people hating on me for a change."

My mom laughs loudly as she reaches across the passenger's side reassuringly rubbing my forearm. "Jayd, with or without those powerful brown eyes, you'd still be a gorgeous, intelligent, fierce girl. And you're from the hood at a nearly all-white school, which means you have a lot of swag. You'll always be talked about whether you like it or not. And high school is just the beginning. From this point on every relationship, job or other school you deal with will remind you of being a teenager. The haters may get older and more stealthlike, but the game is the same. So, stop whining because everyone doesn't get how you roll. They never will."

"Bye, Mom. I love you," I say, standing up to let her get to work. I know she's trying to help, but I don't feel any better. Misty's a vampire, Jeremy's kissing other girls, and Mrs. Bennett's out for my ass, as usual, not to mention the cheer bull. Normal sounds so good right now.

"Have a good day, baby. And remember, Jayd, life is a

gamble; you win some and you lose some. Whether or not you play the game is up to you," my mom says in her mind to mine as she turns the corner.

"Thanks, Mom." I think back walking into the building. My mom's right. I can't hide from the world or my enemies. There are always casualties in confrontation and with the wars on my hands there's about to be some bloodshed around here.

~ 10 ~
Crapshoot

Makes no sense to play the game/
There ain't no way that you'll win.

—B.o.B FEAT. HAYLEY WILLIAMS AND EMINEM

Running into Jeremy yesterday shook me to my core. See-ing him made me realize how much I've missed my man. I called Jeremy and asked him if he was open to talking tonight. He's busy with family stuff all day and said he'd meet up with me later at the Pier. I'm ready to take a chance with Jeremy and work on forgiveness. It took Rah and I a long time to get where we are, but we're in a good place as friends, most of the time. Relationships in general are a crap-shoot. That's why when I find someone who can pull at my heartstrings I fight for them rather than let them walk out of my life for good.

Mickey should take the opposite approach with her ex-man who's now trying to get her attention by sending Nickey gifts through Mickey's younger brother. When she went to Compton to visit her family today, there was a package for Nickey with tons of clothes and other necessities, courtesy of her ex-man. She called and asked me to help her hide it or say that I bought the items. I told her I can't lie to Nigel and that she should tell him the truth about the clothes and let-ters as soon as possible. After much back and forth while I was braiding hair, Mickey agreed to tell Nigel the truth this evening. Even if she made me look real ghetto in front of my clients, I want to be there for moral support just in case Nigel goes off.

When I arrive at Rah's house, I can hear Nigel's yelling from inside my car. My portable iPod speakers are no match for Nigel's anger. I park the car and run up the driveway ready to intervene if necessary. It must be an emergency if my boy's going off like this. Hopefully Sandy's not here. Otherwise I might start yelling, too.

"Jayd, tell him I didn't do anything wrong," Mickey says, running to me in the opened doorway. What the hell?

"That's a load of shit, Jayd, and I know it," Nigel says from his stance in the living room, without taking his eyes off Mickey who looks scared for her life. Nigel doesn't look well at all. Luckily the babies are still at the daycare around the corner. I thought we were going to pick them up and go to dinner, but I guess plans have changed.

"Nigel, I'm telling the truth. He just bought the baby some clothes—that's it. He feels bad for what happened to Tre." I thought Mickey was going to wait for me just in case this very thing happened. At first I couldn't get my girl to open her mouth, now she can't keep it closed long enough to wait for backup.

"What happened to Tre is that nigga killed him, Mickey, and almost killed me. Is that what you want, a murderer for your man? You want the father of your daughter to be the man that killed him?"

Mickey looks at Nigel likes he's lost his mind and I'm pretty sure if he hasn't he's definitely on his way there. He turned his world upside down for Mickey and his feelings of betrayal are well founded even if they may be slightly misinterpreted.

"No, Nigel. You're the only one for me, baby. You know that." Now, I can't testify to that because I'm not sure if it's true, but I know Mickey's not trying to get back with her ex-man over Nigel. I'm pretty sure she's learned that lesson by now.

"Lies, Mickey! It's all a bunch of lies," Nigel says, walking through the living room and toward the back of the house into the bedroom he, Mickey, and Nickey share slamming the door.

I hope he doesn't start throwing Mickey's stuff into the hallway like she did when Sandy was ungracefully kicked out of Rah's crib. Karma's a bitch and unfortunately my girl's definitely got some coming her way for the way she's been mistreating her relationship with Nigel. She may not be creeping with her ex-man, but she's definitely not the most faithful broad on the block, either.

"Mickey, why don't we go pick up Rahima and Nickey and let Nigel cool down a bit," I say, looking at the clock on the DVD player across the room. Rah should be meeting us soon at the restaurant with his little brother, Kamal, who's been spending more time at their grandparents' house in Compton because of Rah's busy schedule. I know he misses his little brother and I miss Kamal's presence, too.

"I'm not going anywhere until Nigel sees I'm not lying, Jayd," Mickey says desperately. "I never asked that fool for nothing. He started sending me letters from lockup and what was I supposed to do? Send them back?"

"Well, you could have ignored them," I say, looking back toward my car. They really should consider getting the broken screen door replaced. This is the only house on the nice block that looks like it needs some tender loving care.

"I almost died because of you," Nigel says, coming back into the hallway with pillows and a comforter. What's he doing?

"I know, baby, and I'm sorry about that," Mickey says, pleading with Nigel, but it's no use. His head's too hot to give a damn about Mickey's excuses.

"I left my house for you, defending you in front of my mama and my dad," Nigel says, making up the couch like I do at my mom's. "What pisses me off most is that she was right about you. Always was." Now that was a low blow. Mrs. Esop has called Mickey everything under the sun from a whore to a goldigger and will probably create some new words for her before it's all said and done.

"Nigel, you don't mean that," Mickey says, crying. She runs up to Nigel and tries to hug him, but he shrugs his shoulders away from her touch.

"Don't," Nigel says, throwing the remaining linens on the couch and laying down. "I need to be alone. Tell Rah I'll hit him up later. We've got some business to take care of."

"You're not coming to dinner?" Mickey asks, seeing her world vanish before her eyes. I know she's regretting taking the outfits from her ex now. I tried to tell her, but she rarely listens to a word I have to say. Maybe now she'll humble herself to help when it's offered no matter how cute the clothes are.

"Hell no," Nigel says, turning the television volume up so loud conversation is impossible. Defeated, Mickey walks outside and I follow closing the door behind me.

Nigel's sacrificed way more than any other dude would've for Mickey's selfish ass. I'm surprised it's taken him this long to check her. The pressure of having to support not only himself, but also a girlfriend and baby has been stressing him out. With football season in full gear Nigel's also under a lot of pressure to perform well for his college future. Several scouts have already come to the games and offered him all kinds of incentives to consider their schools, but so far the coaches at South Bay have protected him like the treasure Nigel is. Mickey needs to learn how to do the same thing.

"I can't lose him, Jayd," Mickey says, walking to her car. We'll take her ride because the car seats are already inside.

"He just needs time to process everything, Mickey. I'm sure it'll be okay." I'm not, but I feel like I need to reassure my friend that she didn't ruin her relationship.

"We're going to find a way to make Nigel forgive me even if it takes all night, Jayd. He has to forgive me." I feel my girl's pain and all, but I've got my own issues to deal with tonight.

"We can brainstorm over dinner, but I'm meeting Jeremy by the beach later," I say, buckling my seat belt as Mickey pulls out of the driveway faster than necessary. I look at Mickey and say a quick prayer to Legba for my safety. Mickey's usually a pretty decent driver, but I think the tears in her eyes are clouding her judgment.

"Good for you and the white boy." The hater in Mickey can't help but rear its ugly head in light of the situation. "Can I get some of whatever you put on that dude to keep my man as whipped as Jeremy is?"

"Mickey, if it were that easy Jeremy and I wouldn't have the problems we've got." Ain't that the truth. No matter how the evening turns out I'm determined to get Jeremy and I back on track. Cameron coming on to Jeremy isn't nearly as traumatic as Mickey and Nigel's drama. And if I'm praying for Nigel to forgive his woman, I should be able to do the same for my man.

Rather than meet us at Pann's, Rah decided to go home and check on Nigel. Sometimes I feel like Rah and I are parents for the rest of our crew. But then again Rah needs my help more often than not so maybe I'm just everyone's mama and I don't know it. Us girls enjoyed chicken and waffles while Nigel, Rah, and Kamal hibernated in the studio with pizza. After bathing the babies and consoling my girl as much as I could, Nellie came over and relieved me as Mickey's nurse so I could meet Jeremy. So far it's been a productive meeting except for the fact he's already high and a bit tipsy. When is enough for him and his crew?

"I'm glad you called. And thanks for the mixed CD. It was perfect," Jeremy says, stopping our stroll and leaning up against the stone wall lining the boardwalk. It's a chilly night in Manhattan Beach where most sane people are in front of their electric fireplaces by now. I've been here for over an hour and I'm ready to get under my blankets with or without reconciling with my boyfriend. It's after midnight, but Jeremy, his surfing crew, and a few other daredevils are out late tonight no matter the temperature. My blood's too warm to pretend.

"You're welcome," I say with chattering teeth. I have on a black pleather jacket, jeans, and boots, but it's not enough layers for a night at the beach. "Jeremy, can we take this discussion inside?"

"What's wrong with a little fresh air?" Jeremy asks, taking a deep breath through his nose and blowing it out through his smiling lips. "Besides, I need another hour to get right before heading home. We can chill in your car if you want." His eyes are too red for reason. This is why he needs to slow his roll. What good is getting bent if it keeps you from moving at will?

"How old were you when you had your first drink?" I ask, pacing back and forth for warmth in front of Jeremy.

Jeremy looks at me puzzled. Damn, was it that long ago?

"I don't know. Maybe ten or eleven," he says, scratching is sandy brown curls under his cap. "It was actually very funny. My brothers played a joke on me and the rest is history."

I can relate to memories of childhood pranks. Being the only girl and the youngest in a house full of boys was always adventurous.

"My uncles put beer in a Coke bottle once and left it for me to drink. I never developed a liking for it, though." If anything my uncles are the reason I'm not attracted to drinking, smoking, or anything else that might make Mama want to beat my ass.

"It's an acquired taste." Jeremy takes me by the waist pulling me into his chest. He's so warm and smells good. Jeremy lifts my chin with his right hand and kisses my lips while stroking my cheek. I've missed the smell of Irish Spring and seawater on my skin, but not the taste of beer on my tongue.

"I don't share that taste," I say, halting the kiss. "Cameron does, Mickey does, but I guess I'm just a different kind of girl."

Jeremy looks down at me in his arms and smiles. "And that's why I love you, Lady J," Jeremy says, kissing me on the forehead.

"I love you, too, Jeremy. But I don't love your habits." I linger in his arms for a moment more and push away from him. I don't want to, but we can't keep going on like this. Something has to give and it has to be Jeremy's addictions.

"I told you I'm sorry, Jayd," Jeremy says, reaching for me, but I reject his approach.

"It's not as simple as that." I wish it were, but like the naval ship out in the distance shining its lights toward the shore we're past the point of no return.

"How can we make it that simple?" Jeremy asks, sounding more sober than he probably has all night. "It was just a picture. I don't even remember taking it."

"Jeremy, I don't have any pictures that I can honestly say I don't remember taking," I say, causing a few heads to turn. I'm probably bringing down their highs, too. "You know why? Because I've never been so high or drunk to even get myself in a situation like that in the first place."

Jeremy looks at me hard, getting the message that I'm serious. "You're not perfect, Jayd."

"No one said anything about perfect, Jeremy. But I'm damned sure not going out like this either."

"So what are you saying, Jayd? Are we really breaking up over this?"

"I don't know, Jeremy. This is all too much for me to handle." I head toward my car, but Jeremy's not letting me go so quickly.

"Seriously, Jayd. It's us."

"I know, baby. But I need some time by myself to get my thoughts together. The truth of the matter is that you were too wasted to explain your actions and that's a problem to me because I can't trust you." It's one thing to party occasionally with friends and another thing entirely to get so high that you can't remember shit. That's how my uncles roll and there's nothing attractive about that.

"Jayd, please. Let's forget about Cameron and everything else tonight and just enjoy being together." Jeremy pulls me back into his warm, strong embrace. I'm tempted for a moment, but I know better.

"I'll holla," I say, kissing the inside of his neck good-bye. Lord knows I miss us, too, but he has to deal with his issues before we can fully reconcile. I forgive Jeremy, but putting my heart back in his hands is a risk I'm not willing to take.

Saturday night was almost too much to bear. I barely slept last night, and with the four heads I had to work on yesterday I'm one tired sistah. Mickey's been blowing up my cell about Nigel packing his bags this weekend and Rah's been on my jock, too. After the long Monday I've had at school the last thing I want to do is go over Rah's and deal with my friends and what could be a reality television show entitled "So, So Hood."

Instead of joining their cast I'm headed to Mama's house to voluntarily work in the spirit room since my help wasn't needed at the shop today. Netta closed the shop to host a workshop on natural hair care for some of her regulars and Mama took advantage of the day off to get some things done for herself. I need to clear my head and be spiritually productive in order to make it through the drama going on around me.

I can't believe Jeremy and I went from reconciliation to forlorn in a matter of minutes. Perhaps it's just not meant to be. Jeremy and I have been plagued with issues since we started dating last year. My heart wants to let him back in, but my mind is telling me to tread lightly. I'm at a crossroads in our relationship and as usual, I need Mama's guidance to help me see straight.

I walk inside the broken wooden gate leading from the front yard to the back to see my uncles and a few of their friends shooting dice. One of my favorite shows, *Unsung*, is blaring loudly through the garage television and they're smoking cigars, enjoying the sunny weather.

"Mama ain't here," my uncle Junior says without looking up from the game. I would ask where she went, but I know they neither know nor care. I might as well head to the back house and wait for Mama to come back.

I see my favorite uncle, Bryan, and have to grill him about his newfound ethical journey taking a left turn.

"Bryan, I thought you stopped shooting craps," I say, smacking him in the back of the head as he stands up. My uncle looks at me and cracks a wicked smile. The other six brothas are still kneeling around the dice. Bryan either crapped out or is taking a break from robbing them of their money, which he's very skilled at.

"Girl, when you're the master it's your duty to school the lost souls." He resumes his bent stance and reclaims the dice before throwing them in the circle. The rest of his companions look sad as he again takes their money. Damn, he's good, but he's always had that kind of luck. Mama says it's all a part of being a child of Legba, which Bryan most definitely is.

"What's up with you?" Bryan asks, leaving the circle and walking me to the small house attached to the back of the garage.

"Dumb shit, as usual," I say, unlocking the back door and stepping inside the welcoming space. I place my purse on the coatrack next to the kitchen table and rejoin Bryan at the threshold. Unless Mama invites her sons or anyone besides me and Netta no one else can take a step inside.

"Sounds like boy trouble to me," Bryan says, reading my mind minus our powerful skills. "Relationships are like shooting craps: you never know when your number's going to get called—good or bad." Talk about a grim reaper. This fool's bringing me down with all this gloom and doom talk. I know he's right, but still. I was feeling all right before I ran into him.

"Man, sometimes you need to leave the unsung quiet."

"Come on, Jayd. You know I'm keeping it real. Shit ain't never perfect, shorty. Even blood can turn on you. You know I'm hated on because I'm the baby of the family and them niggas are my brothers." That's why Bryan and I are so close.

"I know you're right. But still, I can't let it go."

"Not only do you need to let it go, you need to grow the hell up. It's just like throwing dice, Jayd. The odds are against you, but there's a chance you'll win. If you don't acknowledge that you're playing a game you'll always lose. Most of these fools are waiting for you to fall just to make themselves feel better. It may not make sense to you why a nigga would want to trip you, but that doesn't mean you shouldn't watch your step."

"You're just full of jewels this afternoon, aren't you?" I ask, bumping my favorite uncle's right arm with my left shoulder.

"Always, baby. Always." Bryan smiles, rubbing his arm.

"Thank you," I say. I love Bryan and miss spending time with him, even if I'm glad I don't have to give him a ride to work in the mornings now that I'm no longer available. He may be my favorite, but all of my uncles need to get it together and get out of Mama's house.

"No problem, little Jayd," Bryan says, returning the affection. "And you know Rah is your real friend, unlike that white boy you always stressing over?" Why is this fool always trying to push Rah and me back together? I know they're boys but for real, enough is enough.

"Yes, Bryan, I am well aware Rah always has my back." And he does, even when he's pissed at me or me at him. We've got each other no matter what. But like most of the men in my life, he's got his issues, too.

"All right then. You need to give the brotha another shot." Even Lexi comes out of her sleep next to the back door to roll her eyes at that suggestion.

"Bryan, please. The list of reasons why we shouldn't be together outweighs the good so much so I'd have to get a separate piece of paper to keep count."

"You act like your shit don't stank. And trust me, it does," Bryan says, waving his hand in front of his nose. That's one of many problems that come with sharing a bathroom with so many people. There's no privacy.

"Shut up, punk," I say, attempting to sock him in the same arm I just showed love a minute ago, but he anticipates the punch and expertly dodges my advance. I have to take up martial arts with him again one day. He's taught me a few self-defense moves and they've come in handy in the past.

"I'm just saying. We've all got baggage, Jayd. And if a dude's willing to carry yours you should open yourself up to do the same thing for him. Like I said before, real friends are a dime a dozen, shorty. Nobody ever said relationships would be perfect, but they're worth the work when it's good." Bryan's been steadily dating one girl for a while and she's obviously had a positive effect on the player in him.

"Damn, your chicks got you real sprung, huh?" I want to know her secret.

"Yes, she does and I've got her equally sprung. It's a win-win situation." Bryan pats his chest to let me know the gangster's still alive and well inside.

"Whatever, fool. You need to let me tighten those braids up," I say, pulling the ends of his frizzy hair.

"Actually, I think it's time for a change." He runs his hands over his braids and smiles. "I'm thinking of locking it up."

"Word? I can handle that," I say, excited about the possibility. A new project is just what I need to get my mind right.

"Yeah, I'm not sure the wifey would like it but life's all about taking risks and I'm ready." Bryan begins unraveling his cornrows as we speak.

"I say do it. If she loves you she'll respect your hair and love it, too. If not, it's better to find out how superficial she is now before you propose to her." I grab a braid and begin undoing it to help speed up the process. Usually I'd charge extra for this, but I'm in need of the therapeutic exchange myself.

"Ain't nobody said nothing about proposing, but I feel you," Bryan says, running his fingers through his wavy tresses. "Let's do it."

"I'll get my tools," I say, heading to my mom's ride to retrieve my portable hair bag. It seems like I have more natural clients than press and curls these days and that's just fine with me. It takes all kinds and I'm going with the flow. Besides, as long as I get paid for my craft I'll work to please the client.

"No one man should have all that power," Kanye rhymes.

I take my cell out of my back short pocket and answer Nigel's call.

"Jayd's house of hair," I answer.

"Jayd, I'm not coming home tonight. I'm staying with Chance for a while until I clear my head." I think I was too cheery for my boy's sullen mood.

"Nigel, you know Mickey's sorry, but she's in a tight spot. Her ex-man is not exactly the dude you want to piss off." I close the trunk with my bag on my shoulder. Hopefully I'll be done twisting Bryan's hair before Mama gets home.

"But I'm her man now—period. She needs to start respecting that shit or we're not going to make it."

"I hear you loud and clear. I'll give Mickey the message." I hang up the phone and cross the street looking both ways but still feeling slightly lost. How did my crew get so mixed up? Nellie's the only one who's seemed to separate herself from the heat of our collective drama, but she can't live in denial with David forever. Life's all about change and we can either grow with it or fight against it. How hard we struggle in the process is up to us.

~ 11 ~
Hot Combs

And you not hood if you don't know what I'm talkin' 'bout.

—DJ KHALED

School's back to normal with our early Tuesday schedule and I'm glad for it. Mrs. Bennett has been unusually cool since my mom paid a visit Friday to straighten out my residency issues. She hasn't said anything snide to me in two days. I guess Mrs. Bennett's too busy plotting her revenge, which means it's back to business as usual between us.

It's time for Mama and Netta to get back into their routine, too. They needed a day of peace to get the shop back in shape after Netta's event yesterday. I hope Mama's still able to get her hair done. They close down the shop once a week to do each other's hair—no spectators allowed. Usually I'd be there, but I still have several post-initiation restrictions that have yet to be lifted. I'm taking the early day to get some overdue pampering in and the Westside Pavilion is the perfect place to handle it. After I leave here I'll stop by the coffee-house to see how Keenan's doing and get some studying done.

"What are you doing here?" Natalia asks with the rest of her debutante hoes in tow. I hoped I'd never have to see these heffas again. No such luck.

"Whatever," I say, passing them by on my way to the nail

shop. I need a pedicure in the worst way, not another confrontation with these girls.

"You might as well spend your scholarship money on your
nails. There's no way you're getting into a good college anyway," Natalia says, catching my attention.

"What are you talking about? I don't have a scholarship," I
say. The four girls look at each other and then at me, smiling.

"I guess your sponsor hasn't informed you that you were
chosen to receive the Alpha Delta Rho's debutante gift this
year. They always give the honor to a needy girl, and this year
that was you, of course. We can afford our educations."

Money? I won money and Mrs. Esop has the nerve to not
only charge me, but to also try and hide it from me. Oh, hell
no. There's no way I'm letting her get away with this bull.

"No, we haven't spoken about it," I say, feigning my excitement. I can't wait to confront my ill benefactor after my
appointment.

"Well, it's supposed to go toward an institution of your
choosing, but I don't think Compton Community College is
on the list of acceptable schools," Natalia says, her and her
groupies getting a kick out of her joke. I could give a damn
about her snooty-ass comments. I'm more interested in the
check.

"How much is it for?" I ask, disappointing the chicks with
my cool head. It'll take more to get my head hot than a
bunch of rich bitches laughing at me.

"Ten thousand dollars," Natalia says like it's ten dollars.
Goddamn that's a lot of money. Mrs. Esop's been holding out
on me in a big way. I bet she thought she was slick with her
shit, but not slick enough. Legba delivers messages in various
ways and I'm glad he chose the horse's mouth for this special
announcement.

"Why me?" I asked, shocked at the generous sum.

"Every year the lovely ladies of Alpha Delta Rho give away a secret scholarship to some needy girl, and this year they chose you. It was a win-win situation."

"Ten thousand dollars," I say, repeating my award. Whichever college I get into will be happy to see a student with money coming in.

"It was my father's idea," Bridget, another debutante and drunken housewife in the making says. "He's our accountant. Last year the money spent on the 'special' debutante was nearly equivalent to the scholarship, so why not combine them in one transaction, save some money and only have to deal with one beneficiary this year."

That's smart in an elitist sort of way. But I don't care. If there's a check somewhere with "Pay to the order of Jayd Jackson" written on it, I want it in my account where it belongs.

"Okay, so let me get this straight," I say, making sure I heard them correctly before I get too happy about my good luck. "The night of the ball I was presented with a scholarship check and Mrs. Esop accepted it on my behalf?"

"Damn, Jayd. Deaf much?" Natalia asks. This chick better be glad there's more at stake than the pleasure it would give me to snatch her ass up for getting smart. "You won the charity check. Take the pity money and get over it."

"I certainly will." I smile at my little messengers and speed-walk toward the nail shop. I can't wait to tell Mrs. Esop to go to hell and take her bill with her—in a respectful, but firm way, of course. Tricks are for kids and I'm far from playing when it comes to my money. After I get my study on for a couple of hours I'll work on exactly how to get my scholarship money. What's mine is mine—damn the gown.

As powerful as the smell of freshly ground coffee is in the quaint environment that has become my favorite study hangout, the potent funk of someone who doesn't believe in deodorant is even more pronounced causing me to gag upon entry.

"What the hell?" I ask aloud to no one in particular while covering my nose to prevent inhaling any more than necessary. Several of the other twenty or so customers are all wearing the same look: like they just walked into a men's locker room rather than a swanky, West L.A. coffeehouse.

I glance around spotting an empty table in the corner right by a window—the perfect location for me to work. Unfortunately it is also across from a table where two coffeehouse employees are rearranging the shelves. Hopefully they won't distract me from my goal.

I approach the table for one, noticing the stench is more potent over here. I can narrow it down to one of the two people working nearby. Is it legal to come to work when your Secret has obviously told on you?

I set my books and notebook down on the table and approach the bar ready to order. I haven't been here since my vision of Jeremy and Cameron kissing and me and Keenan as lovers in the past. Keenan's behind the bar and welcomes me back with the sexiest smile I've ever seen. Lord help me if I'm not falling for this man.

"Large green tea and a shortbread cookie," Keenan says, reading my order perfectly without me saying a word. I used to do the same thing for our regular customers at Simply Wholesome; it just makes them feel special and at home.

"Exactly." Keenan smiles at me as I attempt to pay for my order. He shakes his head, indicating that my money's no good here and I mouth "thank you," placing the two dollar bills in the tip jar instead. I was already glad I met the brother. Now I'm ecstatic because I've got the hookup, too, as long as I don't ruin it by telling him I want to have his babies.

"I'll come and catch up with you on my break," Keenan says, handing me my tea and cookie.

"I'll be here," I say, heading to my seat. Rather than stay in the direct path of funk I decide to move my table over a few feet. Maybe I'll get some fresh air this way. I place my snack down and gently slide the wooden chairs out first, then the table.

"Excuse me, but I'm going to need to move your table back to where it was so I can clean these shelves," says the funky chick. How about cleaning up under your arms first?

"No problem. I actually prefer sitting by the window anyway, but was unable to concentrate there today."

"Oh, was there a problem with the seat?"

"Actually, in all honesty, the problem was your not-so-fresh odor. I'm not sure if anyone else has ever told you, but you should really consider upping the power of your deodorant."

Keenan clocks out and heads my way. His break couldn't have come at a worse time.

"I don't wear any deodorant; I can't stand chemicals on my body." She's got to be joking.

"They have several lines of natural products that are very good. As a matter of fact, the health food store across the street carries a few different brands you might want to try before coming back to work in a café, you feel me?" We stare each other down. I guess she's banking on people being too polite to say too much about her odor, but I'm not that nice and the truth shall set me free.

"I reserve the right not to pollute my body for the sake of smelling good," she says like she's taking a stand on some important issue.

"And I reserve the right to breathe. And we're not talking about smelling good—we're talking about not smelling like you played a football game all by yourself, for real."

"I wouldn't expect you to understand, but my girlfriend doesn't have a problem with it," she says, obviously thinking I have a problem with her being a lesbian, but I could give a damn.

"Then either your girlfriend is permanently congested or just as funky as you are if she's not lying to save your feelings. You stink; deal with it." Keenan looks from me to his coworker waiting for the next move.

Completely offended, old girl leaves the front of the shop and heads to the back, hopefully to take a bath. The other customers smile at the interaction and take a deep breath of relief. Keenan laughs at my boldness. It needed to be said and I understand she's his supervisor, but I could give a shit about her feelings. We're all suffering and it's not fair.

"I've been trying to tell her about herself forever. Thank you," Keenan says, his sexy smile still in place.

"You're welcome." I take my seat and open my books to get to work. Keenan's break can't be much longer and I don't want to waste any more time. Besides, I have to figure out a plan to serve Mrs. Esop a taste of her own nasty medicine. The sooner I get through to that broad that I can't be intimidated, the sooner I'll get my money.

"Your cornrows are looking good. When I get off work can you finally hook a brotha up?" Keenan rubs his hands through his ebony afro, making me melt at the thought of getting to braid his crown up. Truth be told, I'm afraid to put my hands in Keenan's hair, especially if we're alone. I don't know if I have the willpower to maintain a professional distance when I'm around him.

"I don't know, Keenan. I've got a lot of studying to do." I'm telling the truth, but I always make room for new clients and the money they bring. It's not all about the paper, but I do have a budget to meet.

"Come on, Jayd. Why are you being so difficult when all

you have to do is say yes?" Keenan takes my right hand in his begging with his eyes. When he puts it like that how can I say no?

"Fine, Keenan. You can follow me home." I don't know what I'm getting myself into. Keenan smiles at my surrender and returns to work while leaving me to mine. We'll see what happens later. My toes are done, I'm well on my way to finishing my assignments for the week and I have money on the horizon. As far as I'm concerned, it's been a good day.

It only took us fifteen minutes to get to my mom's place in Inglewood from the coffeehouse off La Cienega. It's cold and dark in the apartment when I open the multiple locks. I flip on the lights and the thermostat, inviting Keenan inside.

"So this is where the magic happens?" Keenan asks, stepping into my mother's living room and bringing his fresh scent of Egyptian Musk with him. He has no idea how accurate that statement is. I close the door behind him and take his coat hanging it with mine on the rack.

"Have a seat in the dining room." I gesture toward the glass table and four chairs off the living room and head to the bathroom to wash up before beginning Keenan's hair. It's been a long day and I want to make sure my Secret isn't giving up the goods like his coworker.

Keenan takes a seat at the table and looks around the intimate space taking it all in. There's not much to see. My mom's apartment's pretty basic and she's not into technology. If he wants to be impressed he should've seen my mom's closet before she slowly began moving into Karl's house.

"All right, let's get started," I say, walking through the living room to where Keenan's seated carefully eyeing my iron hair tools spread across the kitchen counter. I need to clean my collection before resuming my craft this weekend. Depending on how long it takes to finish Keenan's hair I might start this evening since I no longer have plans. I can't believe Jeremy and I are taking a break, but it's not a bad thing I suppose. Like my mom said, I'm young, single, and cute. I deserve a break from being on lockdown just as much as Jeremy does.

"You know pressing hair is reinforcing mental slavery, right?" Keenan says, still scoping the flat irons, hot combs, and curlers like they're the devil incarnate. Mental slavery is Esmeralda and her loyal subjects, but I digress. I don't want to spoil this brotha's head with my own thoughts. I want to stay in this pleasant moment with Keenan.

"I understand where you're coming from, but I don't think it's that deep." I part his soft, thick black hair and feel his scalp. From what I can tell he doesn't need any severe treatment. He must use all natural products because outside of my regular clients his hair is the healthiest I've seen in a long time. I'll introduce him to my line of hair products and see how they improve his already glowing crown.

"How can you say that? You know black women have been oppressed through hot combs for centuries. We need to do away with all that shit in order to save our people." Keenan yields to my gentle persuasion, moving his head with each move of my hands. It's a pleasure to touch his locks.

"Well, I can say it because it's my business to know the ins and outs of my clients. And believe me, there are just as many brainwashed people rocking natural hair as there are wearing it straight."

"That may be true, but that's like saying it's all right for drug dealers to slang in the community because they're actually providing jobs to boys in the hood. The ends don't always justify the means, Miss Jackson."

"That's a little extreme, don't you think?" Keenan looks up at me forcing my hands away from his head. I'm only a quarter of the way done and it's already after ten, making it a late night to be doing hair.

"Look at your beautiful braids," Keenan says, turning the tables on me and touching my freshly cornrowed strands, inhaling their sweet watermelon scent. "Natural hair is an aphrodisiac." Keenan stands up, towering over my short frame. He kisses the tips of my braids moving from the base of my neck, kissing my skin softly before reaching my lips and going for it.

At first I pull back, shocked by his forward advance. But when I pull away Keenan claims me by the waist, slowly kissing my neck, my left ear, and then reclaiming my lips and I let him. It's been too long since I've been kissed like this and it feels good.

"Well, hello," my mom says, slamming the front door. I didn't even hear her walk up the stairs let alone open the multiple bolts on the door. I must've really been floating.

"Hi, Mom," I say, wiping my lips dry.

Keenan attempts to wipe my lip gloss from his mouth, but it's no use. MAC stays put for the long haul.

"Hello, Ms. Jackson. I'm Keenan. It's nice to meet you," Keenan says, walking up to my mom in the living room and extending his right hand.

"I'm sure," my mom says, looking from my last client for the day to me, not pleased. Shit. The last thing I want is to hear her mouth about Keenan.

"I was just touching up Keenan's braids," I say, shaking the towel out and folding it neatly. Even if we're not done it's safe to say we're finished for the night.

"Yeah, I can see that." My mom hangs her purse and jacket on the rack while taking Keenan's leather jacket down.

Keenan smiles at my mom's candor and collects his things, ready to go and I think that's a good idea. If my mom hadn't walked in when she did who knows what would've happened.

"I'll see you later, Jayd. It was nice meeting you, Ms. Jackson." I wave to Keenan who touches his incomplete do. This is the first time I've ever left my work undone.

"Bye, Keenan," my mom says, slamming the door behind my new friend. Usually my mom's not so rude to my guests but for some reason this time is different.

"Mom, it's not what you think," I say, cleaning up. I guess I'll finish his hair another time.

"Really? Because it sure did look like exactly what I'm thinking it was." My mom puts her hands on her slender hips and rolls her emerald eyes at me. My mom's not happy I'm dealing with Keenan at all, but why? She's the one who told me not to settle down with Jeremy when we first started dating.

"Mom, please. I just got out of a relationship. I'm not looking to get into anything else serious right now," I say, putting my hair tools in the hall closet. Going to bed early sounds like a plan tonight if for no other reason but to avoid further scrutiny.

"Well you need to tell that to the college boy who was just in here trying to suck your pretty little face off." My mom heads to her room for some clean clothes and I follow.

"Mom, it was just a kiss." And what a kiss it was. I don't need to look in the mirror to see how flushed my cheeks are. Keenan knows how to leave a great first impression.

"Jayd, look at you," my mom says, gesturing my way. "You're too hot for your own good, girl. I'd rather you lose your virginity with Jeremy than that boy," my mom says, tossing her snakeskin pumps to the side. Is she going to be here all night? Tomorrow's a school day and I don't want to spend the rest of my evening getting cussed out. "At least he's of legal age."

"Mom, it's not that serious," I say, thinking about the prospect of having more than an innocent cerebral relationship with Keenan. From the moment we just shared we both felt the potential to be more. "We're just friends."

"This boy's coming over here at night getting his hair done when you normally stop doing hair at seven. Pretty soon he'll be setting up steady night appointments with you, girl. You'd better be careful with these college boys. They're way out of your league." My mom's got a good point, even if it's at my pride's expense. Keenan may be slightly out of my league, but I can't deny our vibe. "You have enough to focus on without getting mixed up with him."

"You're right, Mom. I'll chill out." I can't forget what Mama spent five weeks drilling into my head. I need to keep a cool head about all decisions. Getting involved with Keenan seems harmless enough, but I need to be careful of my associations, especially with Esmeralda touching so many more people through her lead position in her spiritual house. Before Esmeralda took over the ile Baba Hector, of which Emilio's godfather and his wife had ownership, it was already the largest botanica and spiritual house in Los Angeles County. And with Esmeralda's help, it is on its way to being the largest voodoo house in Southern California. I need to focus on helping Mama stop her and her evil army from taking over. I'll also get Mama's help to check Mrs. Esop once and for all. Keenan and his soft lips will have to wait until after our women's business is done.

~ 12 ~
90220

I won't forget my roots 'cause I don't worship money/
That's not what counts.

—CHAM

Wednesdays are the hardest days of the week to get through, but today was especially grueling. All I could think about was Keenan's kiss the other night. I can't help but wonder what would've happened if my mom hadn't walked in when she did. I've never felt this excited about a dude—ever. It's something about his conscious street swag that's irresistible. Keenan's got confidence that borderlines arrogance—a side effect of him being a star football player for UCLA. I can't stop daydreaming about our next encounter long enough to fold the pile of laundry in front of me.

"Jayd, snap out of it and get to work," Mama says, popping her head out from the office and snapping her fingers in the air. The three clients in the wash area across the shop look around for my grandmother to appear. Most of the people we work with are our neighbors and of course know Mama works here, though she rarely interacts with our patrons directly. That's Netta's job. Mama provides all the background support and I'm their assistant even if I'm not on my job this afternoon.

"Yes, ma'am," I say, focusing on my laundry. I have a lot to ask Mama about, starting with what to do about Mrs. Esop. All of my questions will have to wait until after work.

"There's someone at the door," Netta says from the back porch. She's blending a new leave-in conditioner to use on the women's hair.

"I'll get it," Mama says, walking over to Netta's station and buzzing the visitor in. What we need is a camera by the door. That way unwanted guests like the one who just walked in would be stopped before entering our space.

"So, this is your little shop, Lynn Mae. Cute," Mrs. Esop says, turning her nose up high in the air as she enters Netta's Never Nappy Beauty Shop.

Both Mama and Netta look like they want to throw her out on her pompous ass. Mrs. Esop had better watch herself carefully if she knows what's good for her.

"Can we help you?" Netta asks. She's never one to turn down business, but we don't need any new energy up in our sacred place.

"Yes, actually you can," Mrs. Esop says, stepping closer to the middle of the shop where I'm standing. "Why are you wearing all white, Jayd?" Mrs. Esop asks, distracted by my iyawo attire. When in the shop or the spirit room I have to be in my whites. Netta says it keeps me humble during this period of transformation.

"I was initiated as a priestess," I say, proud of my crown. She'd better recognize whose house this is. Mrs. Esop was once a proud resident of the same zip code. She may not want to admit it, but she knows where she is.

"Oh, I see. Well, Lynn Mae. I'm not sure if Jayd informed you, but she owes me a sizable debt and I think I have a way for her to pay me back without taking on a third job."

Mama and Netta look at Mrs. Esop with all the fury of our ancestors. Mama's green eyes glow fiercely. Mrs. Esop had better back up because Mama's about to blow.

"I owe you nothing," I say, tossing the clean laundry into

the basket and picking up another towel to fold. "You actually owe me ten thousand dollars last I heard."

"How did you find out about the scholarship money?" Mrs. Esop asks, not denying a thing. If nothing else, her swag remains tight as hell—just like the true Compton broad she is no matter her current address. "You're already using your little voodoo tricks to do your dirty work?"

"Actually, no," I say, anxious to return the insult. "It was one of your debutante tricks who told." Mrs. Esop shifts her weight from her left foot to her right, perfecting her bitch stance. She shouldn't dish out what she can't take.

"No matter how you came across the information, it's irrelevant. You still owe me for your dress, not to mention the makeup and sponsorship I provided. The balance stands and is growing with interest every day you forgo payment." Mrs. Esop's Chanel suit is about to go up in flames if she keeps talking.

"Teresa, I'm only going to say this one time and you can take it however you want, but I suggest you take it right on out that front door with your trifling ass," Mama says, folding the towel in her hand and placing it on the chair before stepping to her former sorority sister. "As long as I've known you, you've been a lot of things, but stupid isn't one of them. So it begs the question as to why you would think it all right to come through that door and start something you know you can't finish. Leave now before you get in too deep to escape."

Mama's words still the room—even the usually preoccupied gossiping clients pay full attention. It's not often Mama takes the time to threaten a female. And when she does it's never empty. Mrs. Esop's really on one if she thought she'd get away with this shit up in here. She may be running game over in Lafayette Square but this is our hood. If she didn't know it before she certainly does now.

"Lynn Mae, you don't scare me," Mrs. Esop says, lying through her teeth. "And besides, I have the law on my side. There's nothing you can do about it. But I tell you what, when I take ownership of this shop and everything in it, I'll let you all keep your jobs—on salary of course."

Mrs. Esop hands Mama a legal file. With every word she reads Mama's green eyes slit to almost nothing she's so livid.

"You're suing Jayd for the dress from the ball?" Suing me? Is it even legal to sue a minor?

Netta takes the folder from my grandmother and reads it for herself.

"Actually, as her guardian I'm suing you, Lynn Mae. Pretty soon, you won't have a pot to piss in. Good day, all."

Mrs. Esop throws her cashmere shawl across her left shoulder and walks out of the shop. I can't believe this is happening and it's my fault. Really it's Mickey's fault, but I didn't have to help her by risking my grandmother's life earnings.

"That bitch!" my mom screams into my head. *"She's going to beg for mercy once Mama gets through kicking her ass all over Compton."*

"I didn't see this coming," I think back with tears in my eyes. Mama and Netta are studying the documents religiously. I wish I could do something to help get us out of the mess I've made.

"It's heffas like her you have to watch out for. She's covered her gangster tactics under Chanel, but she's still got a few tricks up her fancy sleeves. Mrs. Esop was comfortable with you in her nice little neat box. She thought she had you figured out and once she exposed you to the finer things in her life she just knew you'd jump at the chance to conform, but you didn't. You, Jayd Osunlade Jackson, chose the ways of your ancestors. She hates you, Jayd, because you are that rare sistah who can be as hood as we get while staying

afloat in the world at-large. You went back to your roots and that, my dear, pissed Teresa Esop way the hell off."

This is definitely the hottest I've ever seen her. Mama looks at me and I know the legal documents are real. How did I get into this nightmare and more importantly, how do I get out? Everything's warped; I can't see my way out. I don't know why my haters keep finding new ways to make my life miserable, but messing with my family's off-limits. There has to be a way to stop all this nonsense without Mama or anyone else getting hurt in the process. The only way I can think of to get an answer is purposely falling into a dream. I just hope I don't screw that up either.

After washing the last china dish in the sink, I place the wet cup on the kitchen towel with the rest of the clean dishes and dry my hands on the apron around my waist. I can tell from the yellow wallpaper and wooden, kitchen table I'm in Mama's kitchen. It reminds me more so of pictures from my mom's childhood than anything I've experienced lately.

I look through the front door to my neighbor's house, which in this case is my mom's apartment, but not current day. The building has been there since the seventies and looks like it hasn't had a single repair done on it since then, too.

"Lynn Mae, hand me a towel, please," Netta says, looking at least thirty years younger. Am I Mama?

"Lynn Mae, are you feeling okay?" Netta walks up to me from the living room and guides me toward the couch. I look back at the kitchen feeling there's more work for me to do but I follow Mama's oldest friend and sit on the couch beside her.

"Yes, just a little overwhelmed," I say, hearing Mama's melodic voice with every word. I haven't been Mama as an adult in a long, long time.

"Well who wouldn't be overwhelmed? You're four months pregnant with your first child, your husband's the head of a new church that you're responsible for organizing, not to mention getting our shop together." Netta's brown eyes sparkle as she helps Mama to her feet.

"Which is why we need to get back to work. We want to have these first batches of our honey-cream oil for the ladies at the church tomorrow. They're going to love it." This must've been way back in the day because Mama and church women don't mix.

"Lynn Mae, your dress," Netta says, pointing to the bottom of Mama's housedress. "You're bleeding."

"No!" I scream, holding my stomach tightly. "Not my baby."

"We have to get you to Dr. Whitmore, now."

Before we can make it off the porch the front door of the lower unit of the apartment building opens and a man comes out. It's Rousseau decades younger and full of life.

"Can I be of any assistance?" he asks, leaping to Mama's side. He reaches for the bloodied hemline, but Netta snatches the dress and my grandmother's arm away from him.

"We're just fine, Rousseau. You can go back inside. We wouldn't want your master coming to look for you, now would we?"

"I haven't had a master in centuries," Rousseau says to Netta while I squirm in pain. "And believe me, he was sorry he ever tried to make me his slave."

"Oh, really? Isn't selling your soul to the devil the same thing?" I ask, unable to keep silent.

"You foolish lady. I never sold my soul to any devil, if there is such a thing." Rousseau's sinister grin sends chills up my spine. If there is a devil he certainly made this evil being.

"*Ha! We know all about you and Esmeralda, Rousseau. You should know better than to try and hide anything from us. This is New Orleans, after all. Nothing goes on in this city without my knowledge.*" *I spew the words almost spitting with every syllable. I have to get to the doctor before Mama gets any worse.*

"*That may be so, Queen Jayd, but you are wrong about me. I just want to help,*" *he says, again reaching for Mama's dress. Netta's not so nice this time.*

"*I said don't touch her,*" *Netta says, taking out a knife and putting it up to Rousseau's throat.* "*Lynn Mae, get in the car. I'll take care of this fool.*"

"*Take care of me?*" *Rousseau snarls, shifting from a tall, muscular man into a dog right before our eyes. Netta doesn't seem the least bit shocked, but I am.*

"*Oh, God!*" *I scream out in both pain and fear. What the hell was that?*

Netta, completely undeterred by the canine's barking picks up a brick from the side of the road and throws it at him, forcing him to change shapes again, this time into a black crow like the one Esmeralda keeps around.

"*Netta, watch out!*" *I scream, panting heavily as more blood drips down my leg.*

"*You evil creature! How dare Esmeralda bring you back to life!*" *Netta swings at the bird with her purse, but misses, all the while getting the shit pecked out of her forehead.*

I get back out of the car, take a handful of stones from the rock garden nearby and hurl them at the bird.

"*Dodge this,*" *I say, relentlessly flinging the stones at the crow who can't take it anymore retreating into a nearby tree. I double over in pain propelling Netta to run to the driver's side. We'll bird watch later. Saving my grandmother from miscarrying with my mother is more urgent.*

"Let's go," Netta says, urging me back into the car and taking the driver's seat. Gunning the engine, Netta backs out of the driveway as something mounts the roof of the car.

"Ahh!" we scream as Rousseau climbs onto the hood, his fangs apparent for all to see. He's shifted into a vampire and Mama's blood is what he's after.

Netta slams on the brakes and Rousseau goes flying backward off the car hard onto the concrete. Thinking he's knocked out, Netta puts the car into drive and speeds away. Rousseau leaps to his feet, shakes his head, and runs after us on all fours like a werewolf. This can't be happening.

"We always knew her people were good at making zombies, but how she managed to bring a shape-shifter back to life is beyond me." What's Netta talking about, making zombies and shape-shifters back from the dead? I can't handle all this new information and my cramping stomach simultaneously.

"My baby," I pant, holding my stomach tight as the pain gets worse. "We can't let him get to her."

"He won't." Netta speeds up with Rousseau hot on our tail. Every corner we turn he turns. The streets look familiar, but the French names don't. I look around in the dark, knowing Rousseau isn't far behind even if I can't see him.

"Shit!" Netta screams, slamming hard on the brakes barely missing the woman in the street.

The stranger stares us down looking helpless in the road. Mama knows all is not what it appears to be.

"Netta, keep going," I insist, but Netta doesn't move.

"I can't. She's not moving and I don't want to run her down, Lynn Mae."

"It's not a homeless woman. It's him." Netta touches Mama's bloodied hand, looks in her eyes and at the woman in front of us. "He knows we won't kill an innocent woman, but we can't take any chances, Netta. Run her down!"

Netta looks straight ahead and honks her horn loudly, but the woman does not budge. "She doesn't even look like she's breathing, Lynn Mae."

"That's because she's not. We have to go before it's too late."

Before Netta can show the broad too much sympathy she smiles, showing her fangs and then leaps onto the windshield cracking it.

"Step on it!"

Netta finally follows Mama's orders and guns the engine causing the woman to flip over the roof of the car and flat onto the street. Netta stops the car and looks behind her seeing a dead dog lying in the middle of the street where the woman should be.

They look at each other in silence, say a prayer, and continue on their emergency. I look down realizing Mama's not bleeding anymore and the cramps have ceased.

I smack the buzzing alarm clock thankful to be out of that self-induced nightmare. What the hell kind of dream was that? Whatever message I'm supposed to get from that is overshadowed by the fear the vision left behind. Being shook up is no way to start my Friday morning.

I have quizzes in every class but drama. My weightlifting class isn't as bad as I thought it would be. If I can't make my way back onto the squad I hope they let me stay where I am. Lifting helps me work off a lot of steam that might otherwise turn into unproductive aggression. And with haters like Esmeralda and Mrs. Esop stepping up their game I've got to be on it if I'm going to beat them at their own games. Mama's working overtime to get rid of Mrs. Esop's vengeful tactic. After school I have to meet her at home to do some special spirit work while Netta handles the shop on her own. I guess we're all in for a hectic day.

There's nothing like a full moon to light up the night sky. Granted we do live in a city with street and porch lights, but nature does a better job at what man tries to accomplish. With the end of the day comes what I hope is the final hour of working with Mama. Me, Netta, and my grandmother have been working in the backyard for the past several hours and I don't know about them, but I'm tired. If we don't quit soon I'm going to pass out right here.

"Jayd, hand me the bucket of spring water, please," Mama says, pointing to the white container next to the Mothers' tree, the primary location for today's events.

"Here you go," I say, handing Mama the water before taking a seat next to the large fig tree. I look across the old, wooden fence into Esmeralda's yard wishing Misty would rear her curly head. But instead, the same bat I saw the other night resurfaces and Esmeralda opens the back door to let it in. Her three pit bulls resume their spots in front of the back door and glance across the yard at me. I've had enough of them to last a lifetime.

Mama notices my concern with Esmeralda's latest additions. "When we were young girls, Esmeralda would call the birds together and chat with them about their days. Imagine actually knowing what caves a bat's been in and what mischief a mutt got into through their own words. It's absolutely amazing, Jayd, as I know you know through firsthand experience."

"You sure as hell didn't want to make her mad, though," Netta says, stacking the last of the mason jars full of different spiritual concoctions into the medium box on the white sheet covering the grass. "When I first started hanging around Lynn Mae in high school, Esmeralda got jealous as hell and sent those same birds after me during lunchtime. The principal thought I was crazy when I told him it was the evil wench and that's just what she intended to happen. If your enemies can't drive you crazy one way, they'll certainly try and find another. Always have your guard up, chile. Always." Netta's right. I got too distracted by mundane shit to focus on the disasters that have come to light. Best believe I won't make that mistake again.

"Spiritual houses war like that, too, Jayd. Churches fall apart over the silliest feuds. It's human nature, plain and simple to want to belong. It's like these silly gangs running around here claiming loyalty to one hood over another. Just craziness, I tell you," Netta says, shaking her head in frustration. Unexplainable violence is a way of life around here.

"Jayd, start cleaning up. Netta and I are going to take these items to the shop. We'll be back in a few minutes," Mama says, walking toward the front of the house. Netta winks at me and follows Mama with her hands full of supplies. Saturday will be a busy day at the shop.

"Yes, ma'am." I gather the remaining elements and stack them neatly next to the tree before folding the white sheet. Feeling someone's eyes I turn around to see Esmeralda's boyfriend staring at me. I nearly jump out of my skin from terror. There's something about that dude I don't like and it's more than his single outfit wardrobe.

"Bon suer, mademoiselle," he says, his yellow eyes piercing my brown ones. "You should really be careful out here at night, alone. You never know what could happen to a beautiful girl like you."

I stare him down just like I did his three canine companions when they tried to attack me, letting him know I'm not afraid to stand my ground. He may scare the shit out of other people, but I know he's just another one of Esmeralda's converts and therefore as weak as they come, as far as I'm concerned.

In less than a second, he's at the gate staring me down. I

drop the clay pot in my hand and it crashes on the ground. How the hell did he do that?

"Like I said, mon cherie. Be careful. You never know what sort of trouble you might find yourself in, especially with a beautiful, virgin neck like yours."

Instinctively I place my hand over my throat, protecting myself much to his amusement.

"Oh, mi petit. I know you know better than that. Nothing can protect you. If I really wanted to get you, I could."

I'm paralyzed with fear, unable to scream or run. All I can do is stare back at him, focusing intently on intimidating him like he's doing me.

"Rousseau, mi amor. Stop toying with the child," Esmeralda says, coming to the door dressed in a long, red negligee. I've never seen her like this before. She looks as young as Mama does. I've never seen Esmeralda wearing anything but large wraps and long skirts. This Esmeralda is stunning, like Oshune in her youth. This is definitely the result of some twisted spell. "Je suis neccissete."

I'm sure she does need him, but for more than being her man. Rousseau is a means to an end. She wants absolute power and his diabolical ass is her way of getting it.

"Your grandmother should've joined by choice. Now we'll have to make the connection for her through you."

"You have no power over us," I say, not taking my eyes off Rousseau for a second. From my wicked dream last night I know he can change shapes faster than I can blink. I'll be damned if I let him get too close to me.

"Yes, this is true. But I do have power over them, and them, and him," she says, pointing to the inside of her living room where Misty, Emilio, and Hector are standing, their collective shadows dancing against the candlelit white walls. From this angle they all appear to be in some sort of trance, and Esmeralda's animals are emitting the same blank stare from their eyes. Rousseau is the only one who seems to be completely aware of his actions.

"What have you done to them?" I ask. I knew she was evil but this is way beyond anything she's ever done before.

"Exactly what they asked me to do. I've made them my soldiers. Your grandmother's never liked much of a following, but I thrive on it. And I needed someone I could trust to make sure my services are appreciated."

"Who better than your ex-boyfriend, the shape-shifter?" I ask, wishing Mama and Netta were here to have my back. It's rare for any of the men to be home on a Friday night and this evening's no exception.

"That's not all he is, dear. He collects payment when accounts are not paid in full, like your grandmother's. And I intend on going after her however I can."

"And I just want to feel the warmth of her neck in my mouth," Rousseau says, growling like the dog he's morphing into. So these really are his dogs. Esmeralda conjured him from the dead to serve as her bounty hunter and her new congregation has given her the ashe to do it.

"It won't work, Esmeralda," I say, trying not to let my fear overtake my otherwise calm head. "Whatever you're planning will fail—I'll see to it."

"You can't do a thing to stop me, little girl. Like the saying goes, if you can't beat them join them. Won't you join us, little Jayd?" Esmeralda asks, reaching her arms out like Daddy does from the pulpit at the end of Sunday service. New members have the opportunity to join the congregation with the support of everyone who came before them gathering around to catch them just in case they become overwhelmed with the Holy Ghost. I'm not sure of the spirit, but I feel like I'm being taken over by something out of my control.

"Place your arms across your chest, now! Make sure your jade bracelets are protecting your heart." Maman's urgent tone leaves me little choice but to do as she says.

I place my arms in front of my body, each fist meeting the opposite shoulder and stare as hard as I can back at the evil wench ahead. The green light beaming from my eyes meets her blue gaze midway, causing the bright light to bounce off the bracelets.

"Such a pretty neck; her veins are ripe and full of their blood," Rousseau says, eyeing my neck through his golden canine glare. I have to get out of here or I might not get another chance to escape.

"Take your time and draw as much as you can without killing her," Esmeralda says, directing her pet without letting go of my sight. How do I keep him down with my vision and fight her at the same time? "We need our mule alive to do our work."

Esmeralda stares into my eyes attempting to break me down with her icy glare. I glare back, mirroring her ice with Maman's powers sending her pain right back to her.

"Enough!" Esmeralda says, closing her eyes. "I'm done playing games with you, child. Marie, I've got a present for you," she shouts at me, aware of my great-grandmother's presence in my head. "Consider it a sacrifice for the queen."

Rousseau jumps the fence in one leap breathing down my neck in an instant. Esmeralda's worn my eyes out leaving me too drained to stare her partner down. This was her true intention all along. All I can do is run. Rousseau and Esmeralda laugh at my attempt to escape, but I keep running, never looking back even if I can feel the pack of dogs on my heels. I look at the crow on the back gate ahead, knowing it's Esmeralda.

I reach the gate, but the dogs are hot on my tail. Before they can move any closer, a loud shriek comes from the front yard. It's Mama back from the beauty shop just in time to save me from being eaten alive. The dogs disappear into the backyard, deterred by my backup's arrival.

I run through the gate and onto the driveway where Mama's knelt over Pam's limp body. She may have been known as the neighborhood crackhead to most, but she was one of Mama's godchildren nonetheless. "No!" Mama screams again, this time breaking my paralysis.

"Netta, call nine-one-one." Mama yells, completely beside herself. Netta runs to her truck parked haphazardly in front of the house, but we both know it's too late. Whoever sliced Pam up like this didn't mean for her to survive.

After almost an hour the police and paramedics finally arrive on the scene. Esmeralda and her flock step outside with candles lit, feigning sorrow, but I know she had something to do with Pam's murder. And her new man is conveniently missing in action. Just then the same bat I've been seeing for weeks circles her house, landing on the roof and eyeing the scene from its perch. I don't know how, but I'm going to get justice for Pam. We may not have an army, but the streets have soldiers and I for one am ready for the ensuing war.

Epilogue

The police were here for all of two hours investigating Pam's murder. After the coroner left with the body, Esmeralda and her crew retreated back inside leaving the cops to question everyone else present when she's the only person they need to investigate. Because Pam's one of several notorious local drug addicts and a black woman, the cops could give a damn about what really happened to her. In their words, they have more pressing matters to attend to than another dead crackhead on the streets. Mama and Daddy were enraged by their response and have been talking to members of the community for the past few hours about what should be done next. It's a miracle, but my grandparents have come together to help see the neighborhood through this tragedy.

"There's a new type of evil aiming to take over our streets," Daddy says from the driveway where the chalk outlining the bloodstained concrete is still fresh. "It's unnatural, cannibalistic. This type of evil can no longer be tolerated in our neighborhood!" Daddy shouts like he's on the pulpit at church.

The crowd stops their individual chatting and focuses on

Pastor James. Daddy can command a crowd with the tone of his voice alone.

"We've taken the 'neighbor' out of 'hood' and there lies our problem," he says, pointing from one end of the long block to the other. "Young folks running around here shortening words, thinking they're original with their revolutionary ideas and feelings of hopelessness. But the mistreatment of the hood by the very people that are supposed to protect the citizens has been around longer than any of us has been alive."

"Well," the church ladies say in unison. I even think I heard Mama hum on that note. She hasn't moved from the spot where she found Pam's body with Netta right beside her.

"Love thy neighbor as thyself. Isn't that what the Lord commanded? Can you honestly say you even know your neighbors, let alone care about them as much as you care about yourself?"

A few people look around feeling guilty for their own reasons. The James' household doesn't have that problem. We know our neighbors all too well.

"If we lived in a true neighborhood sister Pam would be alive, healthy, and strong right now. We failed her, neighbors. We failed God." A few guilty souls lower their heads in shame as Daddy continues his impromptu sermon.

"You may think he has won; the one my wife calls the destroyer. If God has created all of the good things in life, this other evil is the antithesis of God's work. You may think the devil is too powerful to defeat, but I'm here to tell you, God's children, that the answer to these perilous times is right here in this small congregation with a big heart and the favor of God. I'm telling you we, the people of the First AME Church of Compton give our word that we will find justice for our neighbor, Pam. We will find justice for all the nameless neighbors out there who the police have thrown away like trash every Tuesday and Friday of the week." My grandfather's on a roll and taking everyone present with him.

Someone has to make sure whoever killed Pam in cold blood and left her on my grandparents' property is held accountable. The people next door are the first on my list of suspects. Esmeralda will never get away with killing one of Mama's spiritual children, no matter how lost Pam was. Vengeance is Mama's and it will be executed before it's all said and done.

Drama High, Volume 14

SO, SO HOOD

L. Divine

ABOUT THIS GUIDE

The following questions are intended to
enhance your group's reading of
DRAMA HIGH: SO, SO HOOD
by L. Divine.

DISCUSSION QUESTIONS

1. Do you believe in vampires? What fascinates you about these supernatural beings, if anything?
2. Should Jayd give Jeremy another chance? Would you if the circumstances were the same?
3. Do you think Jeremy needs help with his drug and drinking habits or is Jayd overreacting?
4. Have you or anyone you know ever been under the influence so strongly that you lose space and time?
5. Does it surprise you that Misty's showing vampire tendencies and that Esmeralda's trying to steal Mama's blood through Jayd or any way she can? How do you imagine this story-line playing out?
6. If you were a shape-shifter, what would you transform yourself into and why? What kinds of things would you do in your new form? Would you use your powers for good or evil?
7. Should Jayd use any means necessary to get Cameron off her and Jeremy's back for good?
8. What does being hood mean to you? Are you proud of where you are and where you're going?
9. Has anyone in your neighborhood ever been hurt or killed? How does that event affect your feeling safe in your hood?

10. Does Pam deserve the police's attention even though she was a known drug user and prostitute? Should Mama help them find the real killer?

11. Would you go through a ceremony where you were restricted from doing everyday things if you knew it would help you? Explain your limitations.

Jaydism #6

Apple-Cider Vinegar is not only a powerful cleanser, it's also a nutritional powerhouse that helps to lower blood sugar and aids in digestion. It can also be used as an astringent for your skin and delivers essential nutrients to your body all in a small dose of about a tablespoon or two. Whether you add it to greens like Mama does or sprinkle it on a salad, try it out and see the benefits manifest through glowing skin and a diminished craving for sweets.

START YOUR OWN BOOK CLUB

Courtesy of the DRAMA HIGH series

ABOUT THIS GUIDE

The following is intended to help you get
the book club you've always wanted
up and running!
Enjoy!

A Book Club is not only a great way to make friends, but it is also a fun and safe environment for you to express your views and opinions on everything from fashion to teen pregnancy. A Teen Book Club can also become a forum or venue to air grievances and plan remedies for problems.

The People

To start, all you need is yourself and at least one other person. There's no criteria for who this person or persons should be other than their having a desire to read and a commitment to discuss things during a certain time frame.

The Rules

Just as in Jayd's life, sometimes even Book Club discussions can be filled with much drama. People tend to disagree with each other, cut each other off when speaking, and take criticism personally. So, there should be some ground rules:

1. Do not attack people for their ideas or opinions.
2. When you disagree with a Book Club member on a point, disagree respectfully. This means that you do not denigrate other people or their ideas, i.e., no name-calling or saying, "That's stupid!" Instead, say, "I can respect your position; however, I feel differently."
3. Back up your opinions with concrete evidence, either from the book in question or life in general.
4. Allow everyone a turn to comment.
5. Do not cut a member off when the person is speaking. Respectfully wait your turn.
6. Critique only the idea. Do not criticize the person.

7. Every member must agree to and abide by the ground rules.

Feel free to add any other ground rules you think might be necessary.

The Meeting Place

Once you've decided on members, and agreed to the ground rules, you should decide on a place to meet. This could be the local library, the school library, your favorite restaurant, a bookstore, or a member's home. Remember, though, if you decide to hold your sessions at a member's home, the location should rotate to another member's home for the next session. It's also polite for guests to bring treats when attending a Book Club meeting at a member's home. If you choose to hold your meetings in a public place, always remember to ask the permission of the librarian or store manager. If you decide to hold your meetings in a local bookstore, ask the manager to post a flyer in the window announcing the Book Club to attract more members if you so desire.

Timing Is Everything

Teenagers of today are all much busier than teenagers of the past. You're probably thinking, "Between chorus rehearsals, the Drama Club, and oh yeah, my job, when will I ever have time to read another book that doesn't feature Romeo and Juliet!" Well, there's always time, if it's time well planned and time planned ahead. You and your Book Club can decide to meet as often or as little as is appropriate for your bustling schedules. *Once a month* is a favorite option. *Sleepover Book Club* meetings—if you're open to excluding one gender—is also a favorite option. And in this day of high-tech, savvy teens, *Internet Discussion Groups* are also an appealing option. Just choose what's right for you!

Well, you've got the people, the ground rules, the place, and the time. All you need now is a book!

The Book

Choosing a book is the most fun. SO, SO HOOD is of course an excellent choice, and since it's part of a series, you won't soon run out of books to read and discuss. Your Book Club can also have comparative discussions as you compare the first book, THE FIGHT, to the second, SECOND CHANCE, and so on.

But depending upon your reading appetite, you may want to veer outside of the Drama High series. That's okay. There are plenty of options, many of which you will be able to find under the Dafina Books for Young Readers Program in the coming months.

But don't be afraid to mix it up. Nonfiction is just as good as fiction and a fun way to learn about from where we came without just using a history textbook. Science fiction and fantasy can be fun, too!

And always, always research the author. You might find that the author has a Web site where you can post your Book Club's questions or comments. The author may even have an e-mail address available so you can correspond directly. Authors might also sit in on your Book Club meetings, either in person, or on the phone, and this can be a fun way to discuss the book as well!

The Discussion

Every good Book Club discussion starts with questions. SO, SO HOOD, as does every book in the Drama High series, comes with a Reading Group Guide for your convenience, though of course, it's fine to make up your own. Here are some sample questions to get started:

1. What's this book all about anyway?
2. Who are the characters? Do we like them? Do they remind us of real people?
3. Was the story interesting? Were real issues that are of concern to you examined?
4. Were there details that didn't quite work for you or ring true?
5. Did the author create a believable environment—one that you could visualize?
6. Was the ending satisfying?
7. Would you read another book from this author?

Record Keeper

It's generally a good idea to have someone keep track of the books you read. Often libraries and schools will hold reading drives where you're rewarded for having read a certain number of books in a certain time period. Perhaps a pizza party awaits!

Get Your Teachers and Parents Involved

Teachers and parents love it when kids get together and read. So involve your teachers and parents. Your Book Club may read a particular book whereby it would help to have an adult's perspective as part of the discussion. Teachers may also be able to include what you're doing as a Book Club in the classroom curriculum. That way, books you love to read, such as the Drama High ones, can find a place in your classroom alongside the books you don't love to read so much.

Resources

To find some new favorite writers, check out the following resources. Happy reading!

Young Adult Library Services Association
http://www.ala.org/ala/yalsa/yalsa.htm

Carnegie Library of Pittsburgh
Hip-Hop!
Teen Rap Titles
http://www.carnegielibrary.org/teens/books

TeensPoint.org
What Teens Are Reading
http://teens.librarypoint.org/reading_matters

Teenreads.com
http://www.teenreads.com

Book Divas
http://www.bookdivas.com

Meg Cabot Book Club
http://www.megcabotbookclub.com